# MOSAIC OF MYSTERIES

ANTRA

INDIA • SINGAPORE • MALAYSIA

Copyright © Antra 2024
All Rights Reserved.

ISBN 979-8-89544-515-0

This book has been published with all efforts taken to make the material error-free after the consent of the author. However, the author and the publisher do not assume and hereby disclaim any liability to any party for any loss, damage, or disruption caused by errors or omissions, whether such errors or omissions result from negligence, accident, or any other cause.

While every effort has been made to avoid any mistake or omission, this publication is being sold on the condition and understanding that neither the author nor the publishers or printers would be liable in any manner to any person by reason of any mistake or omission in this publication or for any action taken or omitted to be taken or advice rendered or accepted on the basis of this work. For any defect in printing or binding the publishers will be liable only to replace the defective copy by another copy of this work then available.

*"The mind is restless and difficult to control, but
it can be conquered by practice
and detachment."*

*– Bhagavad Gita 6.35*

# CONTENTS

# ACKNOWLEDGEMENT

The creation of this book has been a deeply fulfilling journey, and I have been blessed with the unwavering support and encouragement of many remarkable individuals who have shaped both my personal and creative endeavors. I would like to express my profound gratitude to each of them:

To my late father, **Mr. Rajesh Kumar Singh**, whose love and belief in my potential continue to inspire me every day, even though he is no longer physically with us. Your unwavering encouragement has been the guiding light that has fueled my passion for writing.

To my beloved mother, **Mrs. Anamika Singh**, whose boundless love, strength, and support have been the bedrock of my existence. Your faith in my dreams and relentless dedication to my happiness have been the driving force behind this literary journey.

To my brother, **Mr. Utkarsh Kumar**, for being a steadfast pillar of support. Your belief in my abilities has pushed me to strive for excellence and has been a constant source of motivation.

In loving memory of my late grandfather, **Mr. Arinjay Singh**, whose wisdom, guidance, and storytelling have left an indelible mark on my life. Your love for literature and your profound life lessons have deeply influenced my creative pursuits.

To my dear grandmother, **Mrs. Kamlesh Singh**, for her endless love, warmth, and encouragement. Your presence in my life has brought immeasurable joy and comfort, and your support has been a source of constant motivation.

In cherished memory of my late grandparents, **Mr. and Mrs. Kapil Dev Singh**, whose legacy of love, family values, and cherished memories continue to live on in our hearts. Your influence has been an enduring source of inspiration.

To my uncle and aunt, **Mr. Ajay Singh** and **Mrs. Pinky Singh**, for their love and constant encouragement. Your unwavering support has been a pillar of strength throughout this journey, and I am deeply grateful for your belief in me.

Finally, to my guide, **Rahul Yogi Sir**, for your mentorship, guidance, and belief in my potential. Your expertise and encouragement have been invaluable on this writing journey.

This book is a testament to the profound impact each of you has had on my life and the unwavering belief you have placed in me. Your love, guidance, and inspiration have fuelled my passion for storytelling, and I am forever grateful for your presence in my life.

With heartfelt thanks,

Antra

*In the tapestry of existence, each thread of discovery weaves a new pattern of understanding, revealing the unseen and shaping the path to our truest selves.*

*– Antra*

# ART OF LETTING GO

## Farewell to Familiarity

Emily Carter stood in the center of her childhood bedroom, surrounded by half-packed boxes and scattered art supplies. The familiar walls, covered with her sketches and paintings, felt both comforting and stifling. For 17 years, this small town had been her entire world, nurturing her talent but also limiting her horizons. As she prepared to leave for the prestigious art school in the city, a swirl of emotions consumed her.

Downstairs, her parents were having a quiet but tense conversation. Her mother, Asha, had always been her biggest supporter, but the thought of Emily venturing into the unknown filled her with apprehension. "The city is dangerous," Asha said, her voice tinged with worry. "What if something happens to her?"

Her father, Raj, tried to be the voice of reason. "She needs to spread her wings, Asha. This is her chance to grow. She's stronger than you think."

Emily heard the soft murmur of their voices and felt a pang of guilt. She knew her parents were worried, but she also knew that staying in this small town would stifle her potential. She took a deep breath and resumed packing, carefully placing her sketchbooks and favorite brushes into a sturdy box. Each item she packed was a piece of her past, a reminder of the comfort and security of her hometown.

That evening, Emily's best friend, Arjun, threw her a farewell party at the local community center. The room was decorated with twinkling fairy lights and colorful banners, creating a warm and festive atmosphere. Friends, family, and neighbors gathered to celebrate Emily's next big step. The smell of homemade food filled the air, and laughter echoed through the room.

Arjun, always the life of the party, handed Emily a cup of punch and gave her a reassuring smile. "You're going to be amazing. The city won't know what hit it. Remember, this is just the beginning."

Emily smiled back, feeling a mixture of excitement and anxiety. "I know, but it's still hard to leave everything behind. What if I don't fit in? What if I'm not good enough?"

Arjun put a comforting arm around her shoulders. "You'll be fine. You've got talent, and you've got heart. Just be yourself, and everything will fall into place."

Throughout the evening, Emily received heartfelt well-wishes and advice from her friends and family. Her art teacher, Mrs. Thompson, gave her a set of high-quality paints, and her neighbor, Mrs. Patel, handed her a box of homemade sweets for the journey. Each gesture, each kind word, made Emily feel cherished and supported.

As the night wore on and the crowd began to thin, Emily found herself standing alone, looking out at the town she had always known. The familiar streets, the cozy houses, the people who had watched her grow up—all of it would soon be left behind. She felt a lump in her throat and blinked back tears.

Arjun joined her, sensing her turmoil. "It's okay to be scared, you know. Change is never easy, but it's necessary. You'll do great things, Emily. I believe in you."

Emily took a deep breath, nodding. "Thanks, Arjun. I needed to hear that."

Later, as she lay in bed, Emily stared at the ceiling, her mind racing with thoughts of the future. The town had been her safe haven, but it was time to step out of her comfort zone and embrace the opportunities that awaited her. She thought about the art school, the city, and the new experiences that lay ahead. With a mixture of fear and determination, she drifted off to sleep, dreaming of the journey that awaited her.

## Arrival in the Big City

Emily Carter stepped off the bus and into the bustling heart of the city. The noise hit her first—a cacophony of honking horns, distant sirens, and the constant hum of voices. Skyscrapers towered above her, their glass facades reflecting the busy streets below. The sheer scale of everything was overwhelming. She tightened her grip on her suitcase and took a deep breath, reminding herself that this was where her dreams would come to life.

Navigating through the crowded sidewalks, Emily finally reached her new home: a tiny apartment in an old building nestled between a bookstore and a coffee shop. The building's exterior was weathered, but it had a certain charm. Inside, the apartment was cozy but cramped, with mismatched furniture and art supplies strewn about.

She was greeted by Mia and Aarav, her new roommates and fellow art students. Mia was a vivacious and energetic girl with bright blue hair and an infectious smile. Aarav, on the other hand, was calm and thoughtful, with a passion for sculpture. Despite their contrasting personalities, they both welcomed Emily with open arms.

"Hi, I'm Mia! You must be Emily," Mia exclaimed, pulling her into a tight hug. "We've been so excited to meet you!"

Aarav nodded, offering a warm smile. "It's great to finally have you here. We've set up a corner for your art supplies."

Emily felt a wave of relief wash over her. The apartment was small, but it was filled with creativity and camaraderie. She quickly settled into her new space, finding comfort in the company of her new friends.

The next morning, Emily prepared for her first day at the prestigious art school. She dressed carefully, wanting to make a good impression, but her stomach churned with nerves. As she walked to the campus with Mia and Aarav, the towering buildings of the city seemed to loom even larger.

The art school was an impressive structure, a blend of modern design and classical architecture. Inside, the hallways buzzed with activity. Students were bustling about, each carrying sketchbooks, canvases, and portfolios. The diversity of people and the variety of artistic styles were both inspiring and intimidating.

Emily's first class was with Professor Mehta, a renowned artist known for his demanding yet inspiring teaching style. The classroom was spacious, with large windows letting in natural light and easels arranged in a semi-circle. As the students took their places, Emily couldn't help but feel a pang of self-doubt. Everyone around her seemed so confident, so talented.

Professor Mehta entered the room with an air of authority, his eyes sharp and discerning. "Welcome to your first day," he began, his voice steady. "You are here because you have shown potential, but potential alone is not enough. You must work hard, push your boundaries, and find your unique voice."

The rest of the day passed in a blur. Emily attended several classes, each more challenging than the last. There were lectures on art history, practical sessions on different techniques, and critiques of their previous work. By the end of the day, Emily was exhausted but exhilarated. The intensity of the school was daunting, but it also fueled her determination to succeed.

Back at the apartment, Mia and Aarav were eager to hear about her day. They shared their own experiences, offering advice and encouragement. As they talked late into the night, Emily felt a growing sense of belonging. Despite the challenges ahead, she knew she had found her place in this vibrant city.

As Emily lay in bed, listening to the distant sounds of the city, she felt a mixture of exhaustion and excitement. The first day had been overwhelming, but it also reaffirmed her decision to be here. She was ready to face the challenges, to grow as an artist, and to embrace this new chapter in her life. With that thought, she drifted off to sleep, ready to take on whatever the city had in store for her.

## The Struggle to Adapt

The weeks that followed Emily's arrival in the city were a whirlwind of emotions. Each day at the prestigious art school brought new challenges and self-doubt. Surrounded by accomplished classmates, Emily often found herself questioning her own abilities. The confidence she once had in her small town seemed to evaporate in the face of her talented peers.

During critiques, Emily felt exposed and vulnerable. Her classmates' works were often met with admiration and praise, while her own pieces seemed to fall short. Professor Mehta's feedback, though constructive, only amplified her insecurities. "Your work shows promise, Emily, but you need to dig deeper, find what makes your art unique," he would say, his eyes piercing through her facade.

The constant comparison to others began to take a toll on Emily's confidence. She felt like an imposter, afraid that any moment, someone would discover she didn't truly belong there. Her hands would shake as she painted, and she struggled to capture the images in her mind onto the canvas. Doubts crept in, whispering that she wasn't good enough, that she would never measure up.

Finding solace became essential. Emily started exploring the city, seeking inspiration and a break from her overwhelming thoughts. She spent hours wandering through art galleries, mesmerized by the masterpieces that lined the walls. The city itself was a canvas, adorned with vibrant street art that told stories of struggle, hope, and resilience. Each mural, each sculpture, sparked something inside her.

Cultural festivals were a revelation. Emily found herself immersed in a world of colors, sounds, and traditions. From the intricate dances during Diwali celebrations to the soulful music at street performances, the city's cultural tapestry enriched her senses. She carried a sketchbook everywhere, capturing fleeting moments and emotions, drawing inspiration from the world around her.

Despite her self-doubt, these experiences began to influence her work. Emily started experimenting with new styles and techniques, stepping out of her comfort zone. She mixed traditional and contemporary elements, played with bold colors and abstract forms, and let her emotions guide her brush. Her art began to evolve, reflecting the diversity and vibrancy of the city.

Mia and Aarav noticed the change in her. "Your work is different, Emily. There's more emotion, more life in it," Mia observed one evening as they sat in their cozy apartment.

Aarav nodded in agreement. "You're finding your voice. Don't be afraid to push further."

Their encouragement meant the world to Emily. It gave her the strength to keep going, to face her fears and doubts head-on. Slowly, she started to see progress. Her pieces received more positive feedback, and Professor Mehta's critiques became more encouraging. "You're starting to break through, Emily. Keep exploring, keep challenging yourself," he remarked one day, a hint of a smile on his usually stern face.

As the days turned into weeks, Emily's struggle began to feel less daunting. She realized that every artist had their journey, their battles with self-doubt. It was part of the process, a necessary step towards growth. The city, with its endless sources of inspiration, had become her muse, helping her discover new depths within herself.

Emily still had moments of uncertainty, but she no longer let them paralyze her. She embraced the challenge, knowing that it was pushing her to become a better artist. The struggle to adapt had transformed into a journey of self-discovery and creative exploration, one that she was now eager to continue.

## The Breakthrough

Emily's hard work and exploration began to bear fruit as the weeks passed. The struggles that had once seemed insurmountable now felt like stepping stones toward something greater. Her days were filled with intense focus and experimentation, and it was during one of her late-night studio sessions that her breakthrough came.

One afternoon, Professor Mehta, known for his keen eye and discerning taste, happened to visit the studio to review student works. He paused before Emily's easel, captivated by the painting she was working on. It was a vibrant and chaotic piece, full of bold colors and dynamic brushstrokes that seemed to tell a story of transformation and struggle.

"Interesting," Professor Mehta remarked, his gaze fixed on the canvas. "There's something raw and powerful about your work. I see potential."

Emily's heart skipped a beat. The thought that someone like Professor Mehta, whose reputation preceded him, would notice her was both thrilling and terrifying. "Thank you, sir," she said, her voice trembling slightly. "I'm just trying to find my voice."

Professor Mehta studied her for a moment longer, then nodded. "I see that. And I believe you're on the right path. Would you be interested in working closely with me? I'd like to help you refine your style and develop your artistic voice."

The offer took Emily by surprise. It was an opportunity she had only dreamed of, and she accepted eagerly. Under Professor Mehta's mentorship, Emily's artistic journey took a new direction. Mehta encouraged her to delve deeper into her own experiences, blending the nostalgic elements of her small-town roots with the vibrant, sometimes overwhelming energy of the city.

Their sessions were intense and transformative. Mehta pushed Emily to experiment with new techniques, to confront her fears, and to break free from the constraints she had previously imposed on herself. He introduced her to new perspectives, urging her to incorporate elements of her upbringing into her work while embracing the boldness and innovation that the city inspired.

As Emily's confidence grew, so did her work. She began a series of paintings that she titled "The Art of Letting Go." Each piece reflected a different stage of her journey—her departure from her small town, the initial struggles in the city, and ultimately, her emergence as an artist with a unique voice. The series combined the simplicity and warmth of her past with the complexity and intensity of her present.

The paintings were a mix of vibrant abstracts and poignant imagery. Some pieces depicted scenes of her hometown—familiar landscapes and comforting colors—while others were infused with the chaotic energy of the city. The contrast between the two worlds created a powerful visual narrative, showcasing her growth and transformation.

Emily's series received enthusiastic praise during an internal exhibition at the art school. The works were displayed in a prominent gallery space, drawing significant attention from students, faculty, and visiting art critics. Professor Mehta proudly introduced Emily's work, highlighting the emotional depth and technical skill she had achieved.

"This series," Mehta announced to the gathered crowd, "is a testament to Emily's journey—a journey of letting go of the familiar and embracing the unknown. It is a reflection of her growth, her struggles, and ultimately, her triumphs."

Emily stood beside her paintings, feeling a mix of pride and humility. As people gathered around her work, discussing and admiring it, she felt a profound sense of accomplishment. The validation from her mentor, peers, and the art community was a powerful affirmation of her hard work and dedication.

That evening, as she walked home through the city streets, Emily felt a renewed sense of purpose. The city, which had once seemed overwhelming and intimidating, now felt like a canvas full of possibilities. Her journey of self-discovery and artistic growth had led her to a place where she could confidently express her voice, blending the old and the new, the familiar and the unfamiliar.

The breakthrough was not just in her art but in her own sense of identity. Emily had learned to embrace her past while forging her path forward. With each brushstroke, she continued to let go of her doubts and fears, painting her way into a future filled with endless possibilities.

## Challenges and Setbacks

As Emily's art gained recognition, the pressure to succeed mounted. The acclaim she had enjoyed was not without its challenges. The journey of artistic growth is often fraught with hurdles, and Emily found herself facing a series of setbacks that tested her resolve.

One of the first major blows came in the form of a harsh critique from a prominent art critic, Julian Reddy. Emily had submitted her series "The Art of Letting Go" for review, hoping it would be well-received. Instead, Julian's critique was scathing. He dismissed her work as derivative, accusing her of lacking originality and depth. His comments cut deeply, causing Emily to question her artistic vision and abilities.

"It's hard not to let it get to you," Professor Mehta said during their next meeting, sensing Emily's frustration. "Criticism is part of the process, but it's also an opportunity to grow. Use it to push yourself further, not to doubt your path."

Emily nodded, but the sting of Julian's words lingered. The critical review shook her confidence, making her question whether she had truly found her voice or if she was merely mimicking others.

Compounding her distress were growing tensions with her roommates, Mia and Aarav. The trio had always been close, but their differing artistic visions started to create friction. Mia, who had a more commercial approach to her art, and Aarav, who was deeply rooted in traditional techniques, found themselves at odds with Emily's evolving style. Discussions about art often turned into heated arguments, and creative differences led to a falling out.

One evening, after a particularly intense disagreement, Mia stormed out of the apartment. Emily sat alone in the dimly lit room, feeling the weight of both personal and artistic struggles. Her once vibrant and supportive living space now felt suffocating and hostile.

"I can't believe it's come to this," Emily said to herself, staring at the unfinished canvases stacked against the wall. "Maybe I made a mistake coming here."

The overwhelming pressures of the city and the art world began to take their toll. Emily questioned her decision to leave her small town and the safety of her previous life. The city, which had once promised endless opportunities, now seemed like a labyrinth of challenges and uncertainties.

"Maybe I should go back," she mused, feeling a pang of homesickness. "Maybe it was a mistake to leave everything behind."

One particularly rough night, Emily packed a small bag with her essentials, considering a spontaneous return to her hometown. She wandered through the quiet streets of the city, reflecting on her journey. The bright lights of the city, which had once inspired her, now felt harsh and unwelcoming.

In her solitude, Emily found herself at a crossroads. The thought of returning home was tempting, a way to escape the pressures and criticism. But deep down, she knew that giving up would mean abandoning not only her dreams but also the progress she had made.

Early the next morning, as the sun began to rise over the city, Emily sat down and wrote a letter to her parents. She poured out her feelings of doubt and uncertainty, expressing her fear of failure and her longing for the familiarity of home. In the letter, she explained her struggles but also her commitment to facing them.

After writing the letter, Emily decided to reach out to Professor Mehta for guidance. She needed to find a way to move forward, to navigate through the challenges that seemed insurmountable.

"Professor Mehta," she began, her voice shaky during their meeting, "I'm struggling. I don't know if I'm cut out for this. Maybe I should go back home."

Mehta listened attentively, his expression thoughtful. "Emily, doubt and setbacks are part of every artist's journey. The key is to confront them, not to run away. The pressures you're facing are a sign that you're on the right path. Use this as a chance to reflect, to refine your approach, and to grow stronger."

His words provided a glimmer of hope. Though Emily still felt overwhelmed, she understood that setbacks were part of the creative process. She realized that the path to artistic growth was rarely smooth and that facing these challenges head-on was essential to her development.

That night, Emily sat in her studio, surrounded by her work. The once-daunting task of continuing seemed a bit more manageable. She decided to take Mehta's advice, focusing on her art with renewed determination. The city was still overwhelming, but it was also filled with opportunities for growth and discovery.

With each brushstroke, Emily began to rebuild her confidence. She faced her fears, embracing the complexity of her journey, and slowly started to mend the relationships that had strained. The road ahead was uncertain, but Emily was ready to confront the challenges and continue her journey of self-discovery and artistic exploration.

## Finding Inner Strength

The city's relentless pace and the weight of recent setbacks left Emily feeling drained. Seeking solace and a sense of purpose, she decided to visit a local community center that she had heard about from a fellow student. The center was known for its outreach programs, offering support and education to underprivileged children in the city.

Walking through the doors of the community center, Emily felt a sense of calm wash over her. The walls were adorned with colorful murals created by the children, their vibrant hues and playful designs a stark contrast to the city's grayness. She approached the coordinator, Ms. Priya, and offered to volunteer her time teaching art classes.

Ms. Priya welcomed Emily with open arms. "We're always looking for volunteers," she said with a warm smile. "The kids would love to learn from someone with your background."

Emily began teaching art classes on weekends. Initially, the experience was humbling. The children were eager but had limited resources. They worked with basic materials—crayons, markers, and scraps of paper—creating art that was simple yet full of imagination.

As Emily guided the children through their projects, she was struck by their enthusiasm and creativity. Their joy in creating something from nothing reminded her of her own early days with art. She realized that art wasn't just about personal expression or achieving success; it was also about connecting with others and making a difference.

One Saturday afternoon, Emily organized a small exhibition of the children's artwork. The event was held in the community center's main hall, decorated with their colorful creations. The pride and excitement on the children's faces as they showcased their work to their families was deeply moving.

Seeing the impact her presence had on these young lives reignited Emily's passion for art. It reminded her of why she had pursued this path in the first place—not just for personal fulfillment but to share her love of art with others. The experience helped her see her work in a new light, bringing a renewed sense of purpose and joy to her creative process.

With this newfound perspective, Emily also began to reconsider her strained relationships with Mia and Aarav. The creative differences that had caused friction seemed less significant in the context of the community center's impact. She realized the importance of collaboration and support, both in art and in life.

One evening, after a particularly rewarding day at the community center, Emily reached out to Mia and Aarav. She invited them to meet at a local café, hoping to address their differences and mend their strained friendship.

Mia and Aarav arrived, their faces reflecting a mix of curiosity and concern. Emily took a deep breath, gathering her thoughts. "I want to apologize for how things have been between us," she began. "I've been going through a tough time, and I let my frustrations get in the way of our friendship."

Mia's expression softened. "We've all been under a lot of pressure," she said. "I'm sorry, too. I didn't realize how much my approach was affecting you."

Aarav nodded in agreement. "We've always supported each other, and we should continue to do so. Maybe we can find a way to work together, blending our different styles and perspectives."

The conversation marked the beginning of a healing process. Emily, Mia, and Aarav discussed their creative differences openly, finding common ground and respecting each other's artistic visions. They agreed to collaborate on a project that combined their unique styles, allowing each of them to contribute their strengths while learning from one another.

As they worked together, Emily felt a renewed sense of camaraderie and support. The collaboration was both challenging and rewarding, pushing each of them to grow as artists while strengthening their friendship. The experience underscored the value of collaboration and mutual respect in the creative process.

Emily's time at the community center and her reconciliation with Mia and Aarav brought clarity and strength to her journey. She had rediscovered her love for art and the importance of sharing her talents with others. The setbacks and challenges she faced had become stepping stones to deeper understanding and growth.

With a renewed sense of purpose and a strengthened support system, Emily continued her artistic journey with confidence. She embraced the city's chaos and creativity, blending her past experiences with her present discoveries. The lessons learned from teaching, collaborating, and reconnecting had transformed her approach to art and life, setting her on a path of continued growth and fulfillment.

## The Exhibition

The annual exhibition at the art school was one of the most anticipated events of the year. It was a prestigious showcase that drew influential art critics, gallery owners, and art enthusiasts from across the city. For Emily, being selected to participate in the exhibition was a significant milestone, marking a culmination of her hard work and personal growth.

As the exhibition date approached, Emily felt a mix of excitement and nervousness. Her series, "The Art of Letting Go," would be prominently featured, and the prospect of having her work displayed in such a prestigious venue was both thrilling and daunting. The exhibition promised to be an opportunity to share her journey with a broader audience and to receive feedback from some of the most respected figures in the art world.

In the weeks leading up to the event, Emily, Mia, and Aarav worked tirelessly to prepare. They carefully curated the presentation of Emily's series, ensuring each piece was displayed to highlight its emotional and visual impact. The gallery space was transformed into a vibrant reflection of Emily's journey, with the paintings arranged in a way that told a cohesive story of transformation and self-discovery.

The night of the exhibition arrived, and the gallery buzzed with anticipation. Influential art critics, gallery owners, and other prominent figures mingled, sipping on wine and discussing the displayed artworks. Emily's heart raced as she watched the guests enter the gallery, their reactions a mixture of curiosity and admiration.

Her family and friends from her small town were also in attendance, making the night even more special. Her parents, Maya and Ravi, arrived with beaming smiles and pride in their eyes. They had traveled a long distance to be there, their support a testament to their belief in her dreams. Jake, her best friend from home, was there too, his enthusiasm a reminder of her roots and the journey she had undertaken.

As the evening progressed, Emily noticed a growing crowd around her series. Art critics and gallery owners stopped to admire her work, discussing its emotional depth and technical skill. The praise and interest from the art community were validating and encouraging, reaffirming the hard work and dedication she had invested in her art.

One critic, in particular, stood out—Isabella Duarte, a renowned art curator known for her discerning eye and influential taste. She spent a considerable amount of time studying Emily's series, making thoughtful notes and engaging in a deep conversation with Emily about her creative process.

After the initial rush of the evening, Emily found a moment to catch her breath. She stood with Mia and Aarav, sharing a quiet moment of reflection amidst the bustling gallery. "I can't believe this is happening," Emily said, her voice filled with awe. "It feels surreal."

Mia placed a supportive hand on her shoulder. "You've worked so hard for this. You deserve every bit of it."

Aarav nodded in agreement. "This is just the beginning. Your work is touching people, and it's making an impact."

Their words of encouragement were comforting, and Emily felt a renewed sense of purpose. The exhibition was more than just a showcase of her art; it was a celebration of her journey and the growth she had experienced along the way.

As the night drew to a close, Isabella Duarte approached Emily with an offer that took her breath away. "Your series is extraordinary, Emily. I'd like to offer you an opportunity to showcase your work in a prominent gallery downtown. It would be a great platform for you to reach a wider audience."

Emily's eyes widened in surprise and gratitude. "Thank you so much, Ms. Duarte. I'd be honored."

With the exhibition's success and the promising opportunity ahead, Emily felt a profound sense of accomplishment. The validation from the art world and the support of her family and friends underscored the significance of her journey. The city, which had once seemed overwhelming, now felt like a place of endless possibilities and creative potential.

As she stood among her loved ones, watching the final guests leave the gallery, Emily took a moment to reflect on her journey. She had faced challenges and setbacks, but she had also discovered her strength, resilience, and passion. The exhibition was a testament to her growth and a promising step toward her future.

With a heart full of gratitude and excitement, Emily embraced the opportunities ahead, ready to continue her artistic journey and share her story with the world.

## Embracing the Future

The weeks following the exhibition were a whirlwind of excitement and opportunity for Emily. The offer from Isabella Duarte to showcase her work at the prominent gallery downtown marked a significant milestone in her artistic career. As Emily prepared for this new chapter, she took time to reflect on her journey and the profound changes she had experienced.

Sitting in her small apartment, Emily looked around at the walls adorned with her artwork. Each piece told a story of her transformation, from her early struggles to her recent successes. The vibrant colors and expressive brushstrokes seemed to pulse with the energy of her journey, a testament to her growth as both an artist and a person.

Emily's thoughts often drifted back to her time at the community center. Teaching art to the children had been a powerful reminder of why she had pursued her dreams in the first place. Their enthusiasm and creativity had reignited her passion and helped her see her art from a new perspective. It was a poignant reminder that art was not just about personal success but about making a meaningful impact on others.

With a renewed sense of purpose, Emily had decided to stay in the city. The challenges and setbacks she had faced had shaped her into a stronger, more resilient individual. The city, once daunting, now felt like a canvas full of possibilities. She was excited to continue her artistic journey, knowing that the path ahead would be filled with both opportunities and challenges.

Emily kept a strong connection to her roots, frequently visiting her family and friends back in her small town. Their support and encouragement had been unwavering, and their presence in her life remained a source of strength. Despite the distance, her ties to her hometown were a vital part of her identity, grounding her as she embraced the future.

The day of the gallery opening arrived, and Emily stood before her paintings, ready to share her work with a wider audience. The gallery was a beautifully curated space, and her series, "The Art of Letting Go," was displayed with care and attention to detail. The artwork was arranged in a way that showcased the evolution of her journey, from the comfort of her small town to the vibrant chaos of the city.

As guests arrived, Emily felt a wave of excitement and anticipation. The atmosphere was filled with the hum of conversations and the soft clinking of glasses. Influential figures from the art world, along with friends and family, mingled and admired the artwork. Emily took a deep breath, feeling a profound sense of accomplishment and gratitude.

She noticed Isabella Duarte among the guests, engaged in a lively discussion about the series. The validation and support from Duarte and the art community were deeply fulfilling. Emily realized that her journey was not just about achieving personal success but also about finding her place within a larger artistic dialogue.

Standing in front of her paintings, Emily reflected on her journey with a sense of fulfillment. She had faced her fears, embraced the unknown, and discovered a new level of artistic expression. The city, with all its challenges and opportunities, had become a part of her story—a story that continued to unfold with each new brushstroke.

As the evening drew to a close, Emily looked out at the gallery filled with guests, her heart brimming with optimism for the future. The road ahead was still uncertain, but she felt confident in her ability to navigate it. Her experiences had taught her the value of perseverance, the importance of staying connected to her roots, and the joy of sharing her passion with others.

With a smile on her face and a heart full of hope, Emily embraced the future. She knew that her journey was far from over, but she was ready to face whatever came next with courage and determination. The exhibition was a celebration of her achievements, but it was also a stepping stone to the many adventures and creative endeavors that awaited her.

As the gallery lights dimmed and the guests began to leave, Emily stood quietly, savoring the moment. Her journey had been marked by growth, self-discovery, and artistic expression. With each new challenge and triumph, she was writing the next chapter of her story—a story filled with endless possibilities and a bright, hopeful future.

*    *    *    *    *

# WHISPERS OF THE FORGOTTEN

## The Forgotten Village

Puja Kapoor, a driven young journalist with a knack for uncovering hidden stories, had always been drawn to the mysteries of the past. One crisp autumn afternoon, as she sorted through the belongings of her late grandmother in the old, dusty attic, she stumbled upon a weathered leather-bound diary. Its cover was embossed with intricate patterns, suggesting a story far older than the present.

The diary's pages were yellowed with age, and the ink had faded in some places, but Puja's keen eyes quickly deciphered the words. The diary belonged to her grandmother, Meera Kapoor, who had been known for her eccentricities and love for history. The entries were filled with references to a village named "Shivpur," a place that seemed to exist only in the annals of forgotten lore.

According to the diary, Shivpur was a village shrouded in mystery and rumored to hold the secrets of an ancient and powerful culture. The entries spoke of rituals, forgotten customs, and an enigmatic artifact known as "The Heart of Shivpur" that was believed to possess great wisdom. The village had vanished from maps and history, its existence becoming a legend over time.

Puja's curiosity was piqued. The idea of a hidden village with ancient secrets was too enticing to ignore. She read through the diary with increasing fascination, noting the descriptions of Shivpur's location—a place that seemed to be on the edge of known maps, far from the city where she had spent her life.

Determined to uncover the truth behind her grandmother's cryptic entries, Puja decided to embark on an investigative journey. She meticulously prepared for her trip, gathering equipment for research and mapping out the potential locations mentioned in the diary.

The city was bustling with its usual rhythm, but Puja felt a sense of anticipation as she prepared to leave. She bade farewell to her friends and colleagues, explaining only that she was taking some time off to explore a personal project. Her departure was met with curiosity but little fanfare, as the world continued to spin around her.

As she drove away from the city, the landscape transformed from the concrete jungle to sprawling fields and dense forests. The journey was long and filled with anticipation. The further she traveled, the more the modern world seemed to fade away, replaced by the echoes of a bygone era.

Arriving at the rural outskirts where Shivpur was last known to be located, Puja was met with an eerie silence.

The area was desolate, with only the remnants of an old road leading to what seemed to be an overgrown, forgotten path. The sense of isolation was palpable, and Puja felt a shiver of both excitement and apprehension.

The first few days were spent searching through the ruins and talking to locals who had only fragmented memories of the area. Many were skeptical of her quest, dismissing it as folklore. However, an elderly man named Hari, who lived on the fringes of the village, seemed to recall tales of a hidden village and offered cryptic advice about the area.

With Hari's vague hints and the information from her grandmother's diary, Puja continued her exploration, guided by a blend of hope and skepticism. Each step brought her closer to unraveling the secrets of Shivpur, but the path was fraught with uncertainty. As night fell over the desolate landscape, Puja set up camp under the stars, her mind racing with the possibilities that lay ahead.

The diary had promised answers, but Puja knew that discovering the truth about Shivpur would require more than just reading old pages. It would take determination, insight, and perhaps even a bit of luck. With the ancient village looming in her thoughts, she prepared for the challenges that awaited her in her quest for the forgotten.

## The Lost Village

Puja Kapoor's heart raced with a mix of anticipation and trepidation as she arrived at the location indicated in her grandmother's diary. The landscape before her was a stark contrast to the vibrant, bustling city she had left behind.

Here, the remnants of civilization were swallowed by nature's relentless encroachment.

The area was an overgrown expanse of ruins and abandoned land. What once might have been well-tended roads and bustling homes was now a tangle of wild vines, crumbling walls, and forgotten paths. The village's past life was hinted at by the occasional broken pottery or rusted remnants of old tools scattered among the underbrush.

Puja spent hours combing through the ruins, her efforts proving fruitless. Just as doubt began to seep into her resolve, she came across an elderly man seated by a modest hut on the edge of the ruins. His weathered face and gentle eyes suggested a lifetime of stories and wisdom. This was Hari, a local whose age and demeanor seemed to match the tales she had read.

Hari looked up from his chores, his gaze piercing through the veil of time. "You're searching for Shivpur, aren't you?" he asked, his voice carrying a mixture of curiosity and resignation.

"Yes," Puja replied, taken aback by his immediate recognition. "I've been trying to find out more about it. I believe it was hidden away, but I'm not sure why or how."

Hari nodded slowly, his expression clouded with thought. "Many years ago, people spoke of Shivpur in whispers. It was said that the village was hidden deliberately to keep its secrets safe. Those who knew of it did so through old tales and cryptic clues."

He hesitated before continuing, "There's a legend about an artifact—The Heart of Shivpur. It's said to hold immense wisdom, but such power comes with a heavy price. That's why the village vanished, or so the stories go. They say the artifact had to be protected, and the village was concealed to ensure its safety."

Puja listened intently, her mind racing with the implications. The notion of an artifact with such profound power added another layer to the mystery she was unraveling. She had to understand more about this artifact and its connection to the village's disappearance.

Determined to dig deeper, Puja spent the following days immersing herself in the local lore and history. She visited the nearby towns, scoured old libraries, and spoke with other locals who might hold pieces of the puzzle. Each new piece of information added depth to the legend but also introduced new questions.

During her research, Puja learned that the legend of The Heart of Shivpur was more than just a local myth. It was woven into the fabric of regional folklore, often cited as a source of great power that could bring either enlightenment or calamity. The artifact was described in various ways—sometimes as a crystal, other times as a sacred relic, but always surrounded by an aura of mystery.

As Puja delved into these accounts, she discovered references to ancient rites and symbols that were believed to be linked to Shivpur and its hidden legacy. The descriptions were cryptic and fragmented, leaving much open to interpretation.

Despite the challenges, Puja's determination only grew stronger. The more she uncovered, the clearer it became that finding Shivpur was not merely a journalistic endeavor but a personal quest to understand a deeper truth. She felt a profound connection to her grandmother's search and a growing sense of responsibility to uncover the village's secrets.

One evening, as the sun dipped below the horizon and cast long shadows over the ruins, Puja sat in contemplation. The village's history was slowly revealing itself, but the full picture remained elusive. She knew that uncovering the truth about Shivpur would require patience, perseverance, and perhaps a touch of luck. With renewed resolve, she prepared to continue her search, knowing that the path ahead was as uncertain as the village's long-lost secrets.

## Echoes of the Past

As Puja continued her search for clues about Shivpur, she began to experience a series of strange and unsettling occurrences. At first, they were subtle—whispers in the wind, fleeting glimpses of shadows in the corners of her vision, and a persistent feeling that she was being watched. But soon, these phenomena became more vivid and intrusive.

One evening, while reviewing her notes in her temporary lodgings, Puja was startled by a vision of a bustling village square. The scene was filled with vibrant colors and lively activity, but it quickly dissolved as she blinked, leaving her with a lingering sense of déjà vu—sense of past life. The next morning, while exploring the overgrown paths around the ruins, she heard fragmented conversations in a language she didn't understand, and saw fleeting glimpses of people dressed in traditional attire—figures that vanished as quickly as they appeared.

These experiences were both fascinating and disconcerting. Puja felt as though she was being guided by some unseen force towards a deeper understanding of Shivpur. Her instincts led her to a dense forest on the outskirts of the ruins, a place she had previously overlooked in her search.

The forest was a labyrinth of ancient trees and tangled undergrowth. As Puja ventured deeper, she noticed an almost imperceptible trail—subtle signs of human presence, such as partially concealed stone markers and worn paths. Her heart raced with anticipation as she followed these signs.

Eventually, Puja emerged into a clearing and discovered an old, abandoned temple. It was partially hidden by the forest's encroachment, its once-grand façade now partially obscured by creeping vines and moss. The temple's architecture was distinctively ancient, with intricate carvings and symbols that seemed familiar from her research.

Inside the temple, Puja found a treasure trove of artifacts and murals. The walls were adorned with vivid depictions of Shivpur's culture—scenes of festivals, rituals, and daily life that brought the lost village's history to life. The murals told a story of a vibrant, thriving community, deeply connected to its traditions and beliefs.

Amidst the artifacts, Puja came across an ornate chest covered in dust and cobwebs. Inside, she found a collection of ancient scrolls, ceremonial objects, and a beautifully crafted pendant that matched descriptions of The Heart of Shivpur from her grandmother's diary. The pendant seemed to glow faintly, as though imbued with a subtle energy.

While examining these discoveries, Puja was interrupted by the arrival of a woman who emerged from the shadows of the temple. The woman introduced herself as Aanya, claiming to be the last living descendant of Shivpur's original inhabitants. Her appearance and mannerisms were regal and dignified, with a deep sense of connection to the place she called home.

Aanya spoke with a serene authority, revealing that the village's disappearance was a deliberate act of protection. Shivpur had been hidden away to safeguard its people and their knowledge from external threats. Invaders seeking to exploit the village's secrets had forced the community to conceal their existence, preserving their heritage in secrecy.

"The Heart of Shivpur," Aanya explained, "was not only a symbol of our culture but a powerful artifact that held the essence of our wisdom. It was hidden away to prevent it from falling into the wrong hands. My ancestors entrusted me with the knowledge of its location and the responsibility of guarding it."

Puja listened with rapt attention as Aanya detailed the village's history and the significance of the artifacts and murals they had uncovered. The story painted a picture of a people who had valued their traditions so deeply that they chose to disappear rather than allow their heritage to be exploited.

With Aanya's guidance, Puja learned more about the ancient rites and symbols depicted in the temple. The two women formed an alliance, their shared goal of preserving Shivpur's legacy uniting them in their quest. Together, they began to piece together the puzzle of the village's past and its hidden secrets.

As Puja and Aanya explored further, the connection between Puja's visions and the artifacts became clearer. The echoes of the past were guiding her towards a deeper understanding of Shivpur and its place in history. With renewed determination, Puja prepared to delve further into the mysteries of the village, knowing that the journey ahead would be both challenging and enlightening.

## The Heart of Shivpur

With Aanya's guidance, Puja and her new ally delved deeper into the mysteries of Shivpur. The abandoned temple, with its intricate murals and artifacts, became their base of operations. Each day brought new discoveries—ancient scrolls, ceremonial objects, and detailed accounts of the village's vibrant culture. The more they uncovered, the clearer it became that "The Heart of Shivpur" was more than just a physical artifact.

One evening, as they pored over a particularly enigmatic scroll, Aanya spoke with reverence about the deeper significance of The Heart of Shivpur. "It's not just a relic or a symbol," she explained. "The Heart represents the collective memory and identity of our people. It embodies the essence of Shivpur's legacy, preserving not just knowledge but the spirit and unity of its community."

The realization struck Puja profoundly. The village's disappearance was not merely a hiding of physical treasures but a profound sacrifice to protect a way of life. The villagers had chosen to vanish from the world rather than allow their culture and wisdom to be exploited or destroyed. The Heart of Shivpur symbolized their enduring connection to their heritage, even in absence.

As Puja and Aanya continued their research, they found references to a hidden chamber beneath the temple—a place where The Heart was believed to be safeguarded. They followed the clues and navigated through a series of concealed passages, eventually reaching a small, subterranean chamber.

In the center of the chamber stood an ancient pedestal, and upon it rested a beautifully ornate box. As Puja opened it, she discovered a collection of delicate, intricately carved items: ceremonial masks, ancient scrolls, and a small, heart-shaped amulet. The amulet, adorned with elaborate designs, matched descriptions of The Heart of Shivpur. It seemed to emanate a faint, ethereal glow.

Aanya carefully lifted the amulet and explained its significance. "This is the essence of our heritage, a reminder of what was lost but also of what was preserved. It's a symbol of the unity and resilience of our ancestors."

The discovery of The Heart of Shivpur was a momentous occasion, but it also brought new challenges. As Puja continued her investigation, she stumbled upon old correspondence and documents among her grandmother's belongings. To her astonishment, she found references to Shivpur and its secrets, suggesting that her grandmother had played a crucial role in preserving the village's legacy.

The revelation was both exhilarating and unsettling. Puja realized that her grandmother's involvement went beyond mere interest—it was a matter of deep personal and cultural significance. Her grandmother had been part of a clandestine effort to protect the village's secrets, ensuring that Shivpur's story would not be entirely forgotten.

Puja's growing understanding of her grandmother's role forced her to confront her own identity and her family's hidden connection to Shivpur. She reflected on her grandmother's eccentricities and deep knowledge of ancient lore, realizing that these traits were not mere quirks but signs of a profound commitment to preserving a vital piece of history.

Aanya noticed Puja's internal struggle and offered support. "The connection between your family and Shivpur is a bridge to understanding our shared heritage. Embrace it, and use it to guide your journey forward."

With renewed purpose, Puja began to piece together her own role in the story of Shivpur. She understood that her quest was not only about uncovering the village's past but also about reconciling her own identity with the legacy her family had protected. The Heart of Shivpur had become a symbol of her journey—a journey that was now intertwined with her own family's history and the village's enduring spirit.

As Puja and Aanya continued their exploration, they knew that their mission was far from over. The secrets of Shivpur held the key to understanding not just the village's past but also the future of its cultural legacy. With The Heart of Shivpur in their possession, they prepared to delve deeper into the village's history, determined to honor its legacy and uncover the full story of its disappearance.

## Unraveling the Mystery

The search for "The Heart of Shivpur" led Puja and Aanya deeper into the mysteries of the ancient village. Guided by the clues they had unearthed, they ventured into a hidden chamber beneath the old temple. The entrance was concealed behind a thick curtain of ivy, and it took their combined efforts to uncover the ancient doorway.

Inside, the chamber was cool and dimly lit, with the faint glow of the amulet providing just enough light to reveal the surroundings. The walls were lined with shelves holding ancient scrolls and inscriptions, meticulously preserved despite the passage of time. The air was thick with the weight of history, and Puja felt a shiver of anticipation as they approached the center of the chamber.

There, on a pedestal of intricately carved stone, lay a crystal unlike anything Puja had ever seen. It was a translucent, multifaceted gem that seemed to pulse with an inner light. This, they realized, was the true Heart of Shivpur—the artifact that held the collective memories and wisdom of the village's people.

As Puja and Aanya began to decode the inscriptions on the surrounding walls, they uncovered the story of Shivpur in vivid detail. The inscriptions spoke of a time when the village was a thriving center of knowledge and culture, a place where wisdom was valued above all else. The elders of Shivpur had foreseen the potential for their knowledge to be exploited by outside forces, and they had taken drastic measures to protect it.

The Heart of Shivpur, they learned, was more than just a symbol; it was a powerful artifact capable of storing and restoring memories. The crystal held the collective experiences, knowledge, and emotions of Shivpur's people, serving as a living repository of their culture. It had the ability to restore lost memories and bring clarity to those who sought its wisdom.

Puja was captivated by the crystal's potential, but she was also aware of the immense responsibility it represented. As she and Aanya delved deeper into the inscriptions, they uncovered a crucial detail: the crystal's power came with a cost. To access its full potential, one had to be willing to confront the deepest truths and accept the consequences of that knowledge.

Aanya, sensing Puja's inner conflict, placed a reassuring hand on her shoulder. "The Heart of Shivpur holds the key to understanding our past, but it also carries the weight of our ancestors' sacrifices. We must decide carefully how to use its power."

Puja nodded, her mind racing with the implications. She understood that using the crystal could reveal the full truth of Shivpur, potentially restoring forgotten memories and bringing clarity to her own family's connection to the village. However, she also recognized that such knowledge could disrupt the protective secrecy that had safeguarded Shivpur's legacy for generations.

The choice before her was daunting. She could use the crystal to uncover the full truth, potentially bringing to light secrets that had been hidden for centuries. This could offer closure and understanding, but it might also expose the village to new dangers. Alternatively, she could leave the crystal hidden, preserving the village's legacy and respecting the sacrifices of its people.

Puja took a deep breath, weighing her options. The pull of her journalistic instincts urged her to seek the truth, to uncover every detail and share the story with the world. But her respect for Shivpur's legacy and her growing connection to its people made her hesitate.

After a long moment of contemplation, Puja turned to Aanya. "I believe that preserving the legacy of Shivpur is more important than satisfying my own curiosity. The sacrifices made by your ancestors were profound, and their wisdom deserves to be protected. We can honor their memory by continuing to guard their secrets."

Aanya smiled, her eyes reflecting a deep sense of relief and gratitude. "Thank you, Puja. Your decision honors the spirit of Shivpur and ensures that its legacy will endure."

Together, they carefully sealed the crystal back in its hidden chamber, ensuring that it would remain safe for future generations. As they emerged from the depths of the temple, Puja felt a profound sense of peace. She had chosen to protect the legacy of Shivpur, understanding that some mysteries were meant to remain unsolved, their secrets guarded by those who cherished them.

With this decision, Puja and Aanya continued their journey, now united by a shared purpose. They would preserve the story of Shivpur, honoring its people and their sacrifices while carrying forward the wisdom and resilience that defined their heritage.

## The Revelation

Puja and Aanya's discovery of the hidden chamber beneath the old temple marked a turning point in their quest. Inside the chamber, they found the powerful crystal known as "The Heart of Shivpur" and an ancient scroll detailing its true nature. According to the scroll, the crystal had the power to reveal deep, hidden truths about the past and the future, but it came with a profound risk: it could unravel the very fabric of reality, disrupting the delicate balance between the past and present.

As Puja and Aanya decoded the inscriptions, they encountered an unexpected challenge. Hari, the elderly local who had been guiding Puja, revealed himself as a member of a secretive group determined to prevent the crystal from being used. This group believed that the crystal's power was too dangerous and that its existence should remain hidden to protect the world from its potential chaos.

The conflict escalated when Hari and his group attempted to seize the crystal from Puja and Aanya. A tense confrontation ensued, with Puja and Aanya narrowly escaping with the crystal and the scroll. Realizing their quest had now turned into a race against time, they knew powerful forces were seeking to control or destroy the crystal.

Determined to protect the crystal and its secrets, Puja and Aanya decided their only chance was to secure it permanently. They sought out ancient protective rites described in the scroll, which were hidden in a remote part of the forest. However, their journey was fraught with obstacles as they evaded Hari's group and navigated treacherous terrain.

As they worked together to decipher the rites and perform the rituals, Puja discovered her grandmother's involvement in the village's secrets was more significant than she initially realized. Her grandmother had been a key figure in safeguarding the crystal and had left hidden clues for Puja to find. These clues led them deeper into the forest, to a sacred site where the protective rites were to be completed.

In a dramatic climax, Puja and Aanya confronted Hari and his group once more at the ancient site. The showdown was high-stakes, with the future of Shivpur's legacy hanging in the balance. Puja faced a decisive choice: to use the crystal's power to gain a deeper understanding of her own identity and the village's past, risking the potential chaos it could bring, or to ensure its safe concealment and preserve the delicate balance.

In a moment of clarity, Puja realized that true preservation lay not in possession but in understanding and respect. She decided to use the crystal's power to reveal essential truths while ensuring it remained hidden from those who would misuse it. Puja and Aanya performed the protective rites, channeling the crystal's power in a way that honored Shivpur's legacy and safeguarded its secrets.

As the ritual reached its climax, the crystal emitted a brilliant light, revealing profound insights about Shivpur's history and Puja's heritage. She saw visions of her grandmother's efforts to protect the village, the sacrifices made by its people, and the wisdom that had been preserved. With these revelations, Puja felt a deep connection to her roots and a renewed sense of purpose.

The ritual completed, the crystal was secured in a way that maintained its protective legacy. Puja and Aanya ensured that the knowledge they had gained would be used to honor Shivpur's history without exposing its most sacred secrets. Hari and his group, recognizing the sincerity of their mission, reluctantly retreated, understanding that the crystal was now beyond their reach.

## Reflections and Revelations

Back in the city, Puja reflected on her journey with a profound sense of accomplishment. The revelation of her grandmother's legacy and the successful protection of the crystal had given her a deeper understanding of her own identity and the importance of memory and cultural heritage. She wrote an evocative article about her experiences, focusing on the cultural significance of Shivpur without disclosing the full details of the crystal's power. The article, published in a major journal, garnered significant attention, sparking conversations about the preservation of cultural heritage and the untold stories of forgotten communities.

Puja reconnected with her family, sharing the insights she had gained and fostering a newfound appreciation for her heritage. She felt a deep sense of pride and responsibility towards preserving her family's history and the stories of Shivpur. The conversations with her parents and siblings brought them closer, bridging the gap between their modern lives and the rich, ancient traditions they were now rediscovering. Puja's parents, initially skeptical of her journey, were moved by her experiences and the importance of the mission she had undertaken. Her siblings, inspired by her dedication, began to show more interest in their cultural roots.

As Puja stood at the edge of the forest where Shivpur was hidden, she felt a profound sense of peace and closure. She had honored her grandmother's legacy and the sacrifices of Shivpur's people. The journey had given her a deeper understanding of her own identity and the importance of memory and cultural heritage. She recalled the visions she had experienced, the challenges she had faced, and the deep connections she had formed with the past. These memories were now a part of her, guiding her as she moved forward.

With a heart full of gratitude and determination, Puja took a step forward, ready to continue her journey. The memories of Shivpur and the lessons she had learned would always be with her, a source of strength and inspiration. As she walked away from the forest, she felt a sense of peace and optimism, knowing that the future was bright and filled with endless possibilities.

Back in her apartment, Puja found solace in her writing. She started working on a series of articles and a book that would explore the themes of memory, heritage, and the hidden histories of marginalized communities. Her work aimed to shed light on the importance of preserving cultural identities and the stories that shape them. Puja's newfound purpose extended beyond her personal journey; she was determined to use her platform to advocate for the preservation of cultural heritage worldwide.

The story concludes with Puja standing at the edge of the forest, looking ahead with a sense of closure and anticipation for the future. She is filled with a renewed sense of purpose, ready to embrace whatever comes next, knowing that her journey has only just begun. The skyline of the city in the distance, with its blend of modernity and history, symbolizes the harmonious blend of past and present that Puja has come to cherish.

As Puja continues her work, she remains connected with Aanya, who has taken on the role of guardian for Shivpur's legacy. Their bond grows stronger as they collaborate on projects to raise awareness about the village's history and the broader importance of cultural preservation. Puja's articles and book bring her recognition in the journalistic and academic communities, and she is invited to speak at conferences and workshops around the world. Through her efforts, Puja ensures that the story of Shivpur and its people is not forgotten, and she inspires others to explore and preserve their own cultural legacies.

In the end, Puja's journey is not just about uncovering the secrets of a lost village, but also about finding herself and understanding the profound impact of history on the present and future. She stands as a testament to the power of memory, heritage, and the enduring human spirit. The story of Shivpur lives on, carried forward by Puja and those she has inspired, a reminder that the past is never truly lost as long as it is remembered and honored.

* * * * *

# PARALLEL LIVES

## The Mirror's Secret

Maya Sullivan, a 16-year-old high school junior, often feels out of place. At school, she's shy, artistic, and introverted, struggling to find her niche amidst a sea of extroverted, socially adept peers. Her passion for drawing and her vivid imagination set her apart, but also make her feel isolated. She has a few close friends but often finds herself overshadowed by her more confident classmates. Her self-esteem issues are compounded by the pressures of school, social expectations, and her own critical inner voice.

One weekend, Maya's parents decide to take a short trip out of town, leaving her in the care of her grandmother, Evelyn. Maya loves spending time at her grandmother's house, a cozy old home filled with antiques, memories, and stories from the past. Evelyn, a kind and wise woman, has always been a source of comfort and inspiration for Maya, sharing tales of her adventurous youth and her love for art and history.

After lunch, her grandmother suggests they clean out the attic together, hoping to uncover some forgotten treasures. Maya agrees, excited by the prospect of discovering something new and interesting. They climb the creaky stairs to the attic, where they find a treasure trove of dusty boxes, old furniture, and mysterious trinkets.

As they sift through the clutter, Evelyn shares stories about the family's history, pointing out various heirlooms and artifacts. Maya listens intently, her imagination running wild with images of the past. Amidst the chaos, she spots an old, ornate mirror tucked away in a corner, covered with a white sheet. Intrigued, she asks her grandmother about it.

"Ah, that mirror," her grandmother says with a mysterious smile. "It's been in our family for generations. They say it holds secrets and shows you things beyond your imagination."

Curiosity piqued, Maya carefully removes the sheet, revealing a beautifully crafted mirror with intricate designs around its frame. The mirror is large, with a frame made of dark, polished wood, adorned with delicate carvings of vines and flowers. Maya gazes into the mirror, admiring its craftsmanship and the way it seems to glow softly in the dim light of the attic.

As she reaches out to touch the cool glass, a strange sensation washes over her. The air around her seems to shimmer and ripple, and the room begins to blur and twist. Maya feels a sudden rush of wind, and before she can react, she is engulfed in a swirl of light and color.

When the sensation subsides, Maya finds herself standing in the middle of a bustling high school hallway. She looks around, bewildered, trying to make sense of her surroundings. The faces are familiar, but the atmosphere is different. The school looks modern and well-kept, but there's a subtle sense of unfamiliarity.

Maya looks down at herself and realizes she's wearing clothes she wouldn't normally choose—stylish and well-coordinated. She feels a strange mix of confidence and curiosity. As she navigates the hallway, she notices students greeting her warmly, calling her by name. They seem friendlier and more supportive than she remembers.

Throughout the day, Maya notices small but significant differences. Her classmates are more encouraging, the teachers are more engaging, and she herself feels more confident and capable. She quickly realizes that she is in a parallel universe where everything is familiar yet different—a world where she embodies the confidence and acceptance she has always yearned for.

Overwhelmed and bewildered, Maya tries to make sense of her surroundings. She decides to go along with the flow, hoping to learn more about this alternate reality. She attends her classes, interacts with her friends, and takes note of the differences and similarities. As the day progresses, she begins to understand that this parallel universe is not just a fantasy. It's a place where she can explore a different version of herself—a version that embodies the confidence and acceptance she has always desired.

Determined to uncover the secrets of this world and what it can teach her, Maya embarks on an extraordinary journey of self-discovery and transformation. She realizes that the mirror has given her a unique opportunity to see herself in a new light and to learn valuable lessons about her own potential and self-worth.

As the sun sets and the school day comes to an end, Maya stands in front of the mirror once more, contemplating the experiences and revelations of the day. She knows that her journey is just beginning, and that the mirror holds many more secrets and lessons for her to uncover. With a sense of excitement and determination, she steps forward, ready to embrace whatever comes next, knowing that she has the power to shape her own destiny.

## A New Reality

Maya's heart races as she navigates the bustling hallways of the parallel high school. Everything feels both familiar and foreign. Her classmates greet her warmly, flashing genuine smiles and waves. It's a stark contrast to her usual experience of navigating the school day with a low profile.

The bell rings, signaling the start of the first period. Maya checks her schedule and heads to English class. As she enters, she notices that the classroom is brighter and more welcoming. The desks are arranged in a circle, encouraging interaction and discussion. Her teacher, Ms. Perez, who in her own world is known for her stern demeanor, appears vibrant and enthusiastic, engaging the students in a lively discussion about a classic novel.

Maya takes her seat, marveling at the ease with which her classmates participate. She notices a group of students she recognizes, including her best friends from her real life—Aria, a talented musician, and Liam, a budding scientist. Here, however, they seem more outgoing and confident.

During the class, Ms. Perez asks a thought-provoking question about the protagonist's journey in the novel. To her surprise, Maya feels a surge of confidence and raises her hand to answer. The class listens attentively as she articulates her thoughts, and Ms. Perez nods approvingly.

After class, Aria and Liam approach her. They seem the same, yet there's an air of confidence and happiness around them that wasn't as pronounced before.

"Great answer in class today, Maya!" Aria says, her eyes shining with admiration.

"Yeah, you really nailed it," Liam adds with a grin.

Maya smiles, feeling a warmth spread through her. "Thanks, guys. It felt good to share my thoughts."

As they walk to their next class, Maya notices more differences. The hallways are adorned with vibrant artwork and motivational quotes. Students seem genuinely happy, and there's a sense of camaraderie that fills the air.

At lunch, Maya sits with Aria, Liam, and a few other friends. They laugh and chat, discussing their plans for the upcoming school festival. Maya is struck by how easily the conversation flows and how everyone's contributions are valued and respected.

The afternoon brings an unexpected encounter. In her art class, Maya finds herself face-to-face with her alternate self. The other Maya is confident, with a spark in her eyes and a radiant smile. She moves with an ease and assurance that captivates everyone around her.

The two Mayas exchange curious glances. The confident Maya walks over and introduces herself. "Hey, I'm Maya. You must be new here. It's great to meet you!"

Stunned but intrigued, Maya shakes her hand. "Hi, I'm Maya too. This place is incredible."

The confident Maya laughs. "It really is. I used to struggle with self-doubt, but I've learned to embrace who I am and pursue my passions."

The rest of the class watches the interaction with interest. The teacher, Mr. Kim, encourages them to work together on an art project, combining their skills and ideas. As they collaborate, Maya feels a sense of kinship with her alternate self. They share stories about their love for art, their dreams, and their challenges.

Throughout the day, Maya continues to observe and learn from her alternate self. She sees how this version of her navigates challenges with grace, stands up for herself, and supports her friends. It's a life she's always dreamed of, and it inspires her to reflect on her own life and the changes she wants to make.

As the school day ends, Maya finds herself back in front of the mirror in the art room. Her alternate self stands beside her, offering a reassuring smile. "Remember, you have the power to change your reality. Believe in yourself and embrace your uniqueness."

Maya nods, feeling a renewed sense of purpose. She knows that the mirror has given her a glimpse of what could be, and she's determined to bring those changes into her own world.

With a deep breath, Maya touches the mirror again, feeling the familiar swirl of light and color. When she opens her eyes, she's back in her grandmother's attic, the mirror standing silently before her.

Her grandmother's voice drifts up from downstairs. "Maya, are you alright up there?"

Maya smiles, her heart filled with newfound confidence. "Yes, Grandma, I'm more than alright."

As she descends the stairs, she carries with her the lessons and inspiration from the alternate reality. Maya is ready to embrace her own life with confidence, knowing that she has the power to shape her destiny and become the person she's always wanted to be.

## The Hidden Challenges

Maya steps out of the school, the warmth of the afternoon sun casting a golden hue over the campus. She feels buoyed by the day's successes and the newfound confidence she's experienced. However, as the days pass, the initial thrill of her alternate life begins to give way to a more complex reality.

It starts with subtle signs—small cracks in the perfect veneer of her alternate self's life. One afternoon, Maya finds herself at a gathering of students who are discussing the upcoming school festival. Although the conversation is lively, she notices a tension in the air whenever her alternate self speaks.

Later, in the cafeteria, Maya observes her alternate self, the "popular" Maya, having a tense conversation with Aria and Liam. Their voices are low, and the smiles that once came easily are now forced. As Maya approaches, she hears snippets of their conversation—Aria expressing frustration over not being included in certain plans, and Liam voicing his concerns about the pressure to meet high expectations.

Maya's heart sinks. She's seen how her alternate self is revered, but now she sees the underlying strains. She realizes that maintaining this façade of perfection comes with its own set of pressures. The alternate Maya has to juggle high expectations, manage strained relationships, and constantly prove herself.

In art class the next day, Maya notices her alternate self struggling to balance a demanding workload. The teacher, Mr. Kim, has given her an ambitious project, and she's visibly overwhelmed. Despite the admiration she receives from her peers, the stress is apparent in her furrowed brow and tired eyes.

As Maya works on her own project, she overhears a conversation between the alternate Maya and Mr. Kim. The teacher is pushing for perfection, demanding more than her alternate self can realistically give. "I know you can do better," Mr. Kim insists, his tone leaving no room for compromise. The alternate Maya nods, but the strain is clear in her voice.

Later, Maya has a chance to talk with her alternate self during a brief moment of solitude in the art room. She cautiously broaches the subject, "You seem really busy with the project. Is everything okay?"

The alternate Maya looks up, her face a mask of practiced composure. "It's just a lot to handle. Everyone expects so much from me. Sometimes, it feels like I can't keep up with the demands."

Maya listens, realizing that the alternate Maya's life, though seemingly perfect, is not without its difficulties. The constant pressure to maintain an image and meet expectations has led to a loss of genuine connections and personal fulfillment.

Determined to gain a deeper understanding, Maya spends the next few days observing more closely. She sees how her alternate self is caught in a cycle of performance and perfection, where genuine relationships are strained, and personal dreams are put on hold. The alternate Maya is often seen in solitude, working late into the night, trying to meet the ever-increasing demands.

One evening, Maya finds her alternate self sitting alone on a park bench, gazing at the city skyline. The look of exhaustion and contemplation is evident. Maya takes a seat beside her, quietly offering her presence.

"I've been thinking," the alternate Maya begins after a moment of silence, "about what really matters to me. I've spent so much time trying to be perfect that I've lost sight of what I truly want. I'm not sure I'm even happy anymore."

Maya nods, understanding the weight of her words. "Sometimes, the pressure to be perfect can overshadow what really matters. It's okay to feel overwhelmed. You don't have to have it all figured out to be worthy or valuable."

The alternate Maya looks at her with a mixture of relief and curiosity. "How do you know that?"

"I've learned that perfection isn't the goal," Maya replies. "It's about finding balance and being true to yourself. You don't have to live up to everyone else's expectations."

The conversation is a turning point for both of them. The alternate Maya begins to see that embracing her true self and confronting the hidden challenges is more important than maintaining a façade of perfection.

As Maya continues her journey in this parallel world, she grapples with the realization that even in a life that seems ideal, there are struggles and sacrifices. She understands that the quest for authenticity and personal fulfillment is a journey she must embark upon, regardless of the world she inhabits.

When Maya finally returns to her own reality, she does so with a profound understanding of the complexities of life and the importance of self-acceptance. The lessons learned from her alternate self's hidden challenges empower her to approach her own life with greater empathy, resilience, and authenticity.

## The Journey of Self-Discovery

As Maya continues to navigate the complexities of her alternate life, she becomes increasingly aware of the subtle but significant differences between her reality and this parallel world. What initially appeared to be a dream come true reveals itself to be a journey of self-discovery, marked by both challenges and revelations.

Maya starts by focusing on the issues faced by her alternate self. She observes how the pressure to conform to societal expectations affects her alternate self's relationships and self-esteem. Through candid conversations and empathetic support, Maya becomes a catalyst for change.

One evening, Maya accompanies her alternate self to a gathering where she is expected to make a grand speech. The event is filled with influential figures, and the atmosphere is charged with high expectations. The alternate Maya is nervous, and her usual confidence seems to waver. Maya offers encouragement, sharing her own experiences with facing fears and embracing imperfections.

"You don't have to be perfect to be valuable," Maya tells her. "Just be yourself, and that's enough."

The alternate Maya takes this advice to heart. As she delivers her speech, she speaks from the heart, sharing personal insights and vulnerabilities. The response is overwhelmingly positive, not because of a flawless presentation, but because of the genuine connection she establishes with her audience. This moment marks a turning point for her alternate self, who begins to value authenticity over perfection.

Meanwhile, Maya's own journey of self-discovery deepens. She reflects on her experiences and realizes that many of her insecurities and struggles mirror those faced by her alternate self. Maya has always felt overshadowed by others, striving to fit into molds that didn't truly represent her. Witnessing her alternate self's transformation inspires Maya to confront her own fears and self-doubts.

Maya decides to address her own issues head-on. She begins by participating in activities she has always avoided due to fear of failure or judgment. She joins a school club focused on creative writing, something she had always wanted to explore but never dared to try. Through this new venture, Maya discovers a passion for storytelling and begins to channel her thoughts and emotions into writing.

As she writes, Maya finds solace in expressing her true self. Her stories become a reflection of her inner world, and she receives positive feedback from her peers, which boosts her confidence. The process of self-expression helps Maya recognize her unique qualities and understand her own worth.

Maya also extends her support to her alternate self by encouraging her to pursue long-forgotten dreams. They work together to revive an old art project that the alternate Maya had abandoned. The project, once a source of stress, becomes a collaborative effort that strengthens their bond and brings joy to both of them. Through this shared experience, Maya learns the value of pursuing passions and supporting others in their journey.

In the final days of her stay in the parallel world, Maya and her alternate self embark on a reflective journey together. They visit places that hold special significance to them, such as a serene lake where they discuss their dreams and aspirations. They talk about the importance of staying true to oneself, despite external pressures.

The conversations they share are transformative. Maya gains profound insights into the nature of self-worth and resilience. She learns that embracing one's unique qualities, facing challenges with courage, and valuing authentic connections are key to leading a fulfilling life.

As Maya prepares to return to her own world, she has one last heartfelt conversation with her alternate self. They exchange words of gratitude and encouragement, knowing that their time together has been a profound journey of mutual growth.

Back in her own reality, Maya carries the lessons she has learned into her daily life. She embraces her true self with newfound confidence and resilience. The experience in the parallel world has given her a deeper understanding of what it means to live authentically and value personal growth.

Maya's journey of self-discovery continues as she applies the insights she gained to her own life. She approaches challenges with a renewed sense of purpose and encourages those around her to embrace their unique qualities. The lessons from her parallel adventure become a guiding force in her quest for self-acceptance and personal fulfillment.

## The Return Home

The day had arrived for Maya to return to her own world. As she stood before the ornate mirror, she was filled with a bittersweet mix of emotions. The parallel reality had gifted her invaluable insights and transformative experiences, but it was time to bring those lessons back to her everyday life.

Before stepping through the mirror, Maya took one last look around the parallel world. She revisited the serene lake where she had shared deep conversations with her alternate self, the vibrant art studio where her creativity had flourished, and the lively city streets where she had learned to embrace her passions. Each location held memories of her personal growth, and she cherished the connections she had made.

Her alternate self, now brimming with self-assurance and contentment, embraced Maya with a heartfelt farewell. They exchanged tokens of their journey: Maya received a delicate pendant, a symbol of their shared experiences, while she gifted her alternate self a journal filled with reflections and encouragement. The parting was emotional, but it was marked by a sense of mutual respect and gratitude.

As Maya stepped through the mirror, she was greeted by the familiar sights and sounds of her own world. The world she returned to seemed different, seen through the lens of her newfound self-awareness. The challenges she had once felt overwhelmed by now appeared more manageable, and she felt ready to face them with a fresh perspective.

Her first encounter back in her reality was with her family. She embraced them with warmth, sharing her journey and the lessons she had learned. The conversations that followed deepened their bond, as Maya opened up about her transformative experience. Her family listened with fascination and support, and their strengthened connection became a source of comfort and encouragement.

At school, Maya approached her peers and teachers with renewed confidence. She joined the creative writing club she had previously hesitated to join, driven by a genuine passion for storytelling. Her contributions were met with enthusiasm, and she began to gain recognition for her authentic voice and talent. Through her writing, she found joy and fulfillment, expressing herself in ways she had never imagined.

Maya also took steps to mend strained friendships. She reached out to her friends with empathy, acknowledging past misunderstandings and showing a willingness to reconnect. Her efforts to be supportive and present were met with appreciation, and her relationships grew deeper and more meaningful.

Her pursuits extended beyond academics. Maya explored activities she had always been interested in, such as painting and community service. These new ventures brought her a sense of accomplishment and joy, reinforcing her belief in the importance of following one's passions and embracing individuality.

As she continued her journey, Maya became an advocate for self-acceptance and authenticity. She shared her story with others, encouraging them to embrace their true selves and face their challenges with courage. Her experiences served as a beacon of inspiration, and she became a source of support for those around her.

Maya kept a journal to reflect on her experiences and ongoing personal growth. The wisdom from her parallel adventure guided her decisions and interactions, helping her navigate life's complexities with balance and thoughtfulness.

One evening, as Maya walked through her favorite park, the sunset painted the sky in hues of gold and pink. She paused to take in the beauty of the moment, feeling a profound sense of peace and fulfillment. The sunset symbolized the end of one chapter and the beginning of another, marking her journey with hope and determination.

With the lessons from her adventure still fresh in her mind, Maya looked toward the future with optimism. She felt ready to embrace whatever came next, knowing that the journey of self-discovery and the power of self-acceptance would always guide her path. As she walked away from the park, her heart was full of hope, and her spirit was renewed, ready to face the world with a sense of purpose and grace.

## Embracing Change

Back in her own world, Maya felt the weight of her transformative journey settling comfortably into her life. The lessons she had learned in the parallel universe began to unfold in meaningful ways, guiding her actions and decisions.

The first step Maya took was reconnecting with old friends. She reached out to those she had drifted away from, mending relationships that had once been important to her. With genuine apologies and heartfelt conversations, she rekindled old bonds and found that her friends were more receptive than she had expected. They were eager to hear about her adventures and the changes she had undergone, and their support became a pillar in her renewed sense of self.

At school, Maya embraced new challenges with enthusiasm. She joined a leadership program that offered opportunities to develop her skills and make a positive impact on her community. This role allowed her to take on responsibilities she had previously shied away from, such as organizing events and speaking in front of her peers. Each challenge was met with a sense of purpose, and Maya's confidence grew with every success.

One of Maya's most significant changes was starting a blog dedicated to sharing her journey and helping others overcome self-doubt. She titled the blog "Reflections of a Dreamer" and used it as a platform to write about her experiences, the lessons she had learned, and the strategies she had found helpful in navigating life's uncertainties. Her posts ranged from personal anecdotes to practical advice, and she was astonished by the positive responses she received from readers around the world.

Maya's blog became a source of inspiration for many. Readers reached out to her, sharing their own stories and expressing gratitude for the encouragement she provided. Maya took the time to respond to each message, offering support and advice based on her own experiences. The interactions helped her realize the impact of her words and the power of community in fostering personal growth.

As Maya continued to evolve, she also became involved in various community projects. She volunteered at local shelters, organized art workshops for children, and participated in environmental clean-up drives. These activities not only allowed her to give back but also deepened her sense of purpose and fulfillment. The experiences enriched her life, adding layers of meaning and connection.

Her newfound confidence and authenticity began to influence those around her. Friends and classmates noticed Maya's positive changes and were inspired to embrace their true selves. Conversations about self-acceptance and personal growth became more frequent, and Maya found herself in the role of a mentor and motivator. Her story served as a beacon of hope for others grappling with their own challenges.

Maya's family also noticed the transformation in her. They supported her endeavors and celebrated her achievements. Family dinners became a time for sharing stories of growth and success, creating a supportive environment where everyone felt encouraged to pursue their passions and dreams.

One afternoon, as Maya sat in her favorite coffee shop, working on a new blog post, she looked out the window at the bustling street. The vibrant cityscape was a testament to the dynamic and ever-changing world she lived in. The blend of past and present, tradition and innovation, mirrored her own journey—a continuous evolution of self-discovery and acceptance.

With each passing day, Maya felt more at home in her own skin. The struggles and triumphs of her parallel adventure had shaped her into someone who embraced change with grace and purpose. Her life was now a reflection of her inner strength and resilience, and she was ready to face whatever the future held.

As the sun dipped below the horizon, casting a warm glow over the city, Maya felt a deep sense of contentment. Her journey had taught her that embracing change was not about becoming someone else but about becoming the best version of herself. With a heart full of gratitude and a spirit brimming with hope, Maya looked forward to the endless possibilities that awaited her.

In her world and beyond, Maya had found her place. The mirror's secret had unlocked a profound understanding of her true self, and she was ready to continue her journey with unwavering confidence and an open heart.

## The Legacy of the Mirror

Months had passed since Maya's return from the parallel world, but the mirror remained a vivid memory etched in her heart. She often thought about it, its ornate frame and mysterious allure, and the way it had transformed her life. The attic, once a dusty and neglected space, had become a cherished sanctuary for Maya—a place where she could reconnect with the profound experiences that had shaped her.

One afternoon, driven by a mix of curiosity and nostalgia, Maya ventured back to her grandmother's attic. The mirror stood in its corner, just as she had left it, but it now seemed even more significant. Its reflective surface seemed to hum with a gentle energy, as if it was waiting for her.

As she stood before it, Maya felt a sense of reverence. She reached out to touch its cool, smooth surface, recalling the day she had first been transported to the parallel universe. The mirror had been more than just a portal; it had been a catalyst for her transformation.

While exploring the attic, Maya stumbled upon a collection of old letters and journals tucked away in a wooden trunk. They were handwritten by various members of her family, their names written in elegant scripts that matched the age of the documents. Intrigued, she began to read through them, uncovering stories of her ancestors and their own journeys of self-discovery.

The letters revealed that the mirror had been a family heirloom for generations, passed down from one relative to another. Each person who had encountered it had embarked on a personal quest, finding their own version of transformation and enlightenment. Some had faced their fears, others had pursued dreams they had long abandoned, and many had found clarity in their lives. The mirror seemed to hold a legacy of resilience and self-discovery, its power extending through the ages.

Maya's great-grandmother, for instance, had used the mirror during a period of personal crisis, emerging from her experience with renewed purpose and strength. Her stories echoed Maya's own journey, filled with themes of overcoming obstacles and embracing one's true self. Similarly, her grandmother's writings detailed how the mirror had helped her navigate challenging times and find her path in life.

The more Maya read, the more she felt connected to her family's legacy. It was as if the mirror had been a guiding light for many before her, each person adding their own chapter to the family's rich history of self-discovery. She felt a deep sense of belonging, knowing that she was part of a lineage of resilient individuals who had used the mirror to unlock their potential.

Feeling inspired, Maya decided to preserve these family stories and the mirror's legacy. She carefully transcribed the letters and journal entries, creating a comprehensive record of her family's experiences. Her goal was to share this history with future generations, ensuring that the mirror's legacy continued to inspire and guide.

Maya also made a point of visiting the attic regularly, using the time to reflect on her growth and connect with the mirror's enduring presence. Each visit reaffirmed her commitment to living authentically and embracing her unique journey.

In sharing her family's stories with friends and readers, Maya highlighted the power of self-discovery and the importance of understanding one's heritage. Her blog post about the mirror's legacy resonated with many, prompting conversations about the value of family traditions and personal growth.

The mirror, once a symbol of Maya's own transformation, became a beacon of inspiration for her entire family. It stood as a testament to the enduring power of self-discovery and the interconnectedness of their stories. Maya knew that the journey was ongoing and that the mirror's legacy would continue to guide and inspire generations to come.

As she stood before the mirror one last time before leaving the attic, Maya felt a profound sense of peace. The mirror had not only transformed her life but had also connected her to a timeless legacy of resilience and self-discovery. With a heart full of gratitude, Maya closed the attic door, knowing that her journey was an integral part of a larger, enduring story that would continue to unfold.

* * * * *

# THE FUTURE'S CALL

## The Mysterious Phone

Aditya Mehra, a 15-year-old high school student with a penchant for adventure, was sprawled on the dusty floor of his attic, surrounded by relics of a bygone era. The attic, a labyrinth of old trunks and forgotten treasures, was a place he usually avoided. But today, with summer vacation stretching before him and an insatiable curiosity driving him, he had decided to tackle the mess.

Amidst the clutter, Aditya's fingers brushed against something unexpected—a vintage phone, its once-shiny surface now tarnished by time. It was a rotary phone, the kind that looked straight out of a black-and-white movie. His eyes widened in interest.

Aditya: (muttering) Whoa, look at this! Haven't seen one of these in years.

He picked up the phone, examining it closely. It had an ornate design, with intricate carvings and a small, unusual screen embedded on the front. The screen flickered to life, revealing a series of cryptic symbols and dates that seemed both ancient and futuristic.

Aditya: (confused) This thing has a screen? How is that even possible?

He turned the phone over in his hands, trying to make sense of its strange features. As he played with the rotary dial and pressed various buttons, a low hum resonated from the phone. The screen flashed, and suddenly, a new message appeared:

Phone Screen: "Aditya, this is a warning. A crisis is coming that will test everything you know. Understand this phone, and you may find a way to preent it."

Aditya's heart skipped a beat. He stared at the message, his mind racing. A message from the future? This had to be some kind of prank—or a very elaborate joke.

Aditya: (in disbelief) No way. This has to be a joke.

He picked up the receiver and held it to his ear, expecting silence. Instead, a faint, crackling voice came through, barely audible.

Voice: "Aditya, you must act fast. The danger is real, and time is running out. The phone will guide you, but you must be prepared for what lies ahead."

Aditya's skepticism melted into concern. He replaced the receiver, his hands trembling slightly. The message on the screen was clear: he needed to understand the phone's purpose and act quickly. But how could he, a regular teenager, deal with a crisis foretold by a phone?

Aditya: (determined) Okay, if this is real, I need to figure out what's going on. This phone might be the key to something big.

He carefully placed the phone into his backpack, feeling its weight as though it carried the weight of the world. As he stood up, he glanced around the attic one last time. The dim light filtering through the dusty window made the space feel even more eerie, and the phone seemed to glow with an enigmatic significance.

Aditya: (to himself) This is going to be one wild summer.

Aditya descended the attic stairs, his mind filled with questions and a growing sense of urgency. Little did he know, this discovery was the beginning of a journey that would challenge everything he thought he knew about himself and the world around him.

With the mysterious phone as his guide, Aditya was about to step into a world of uncertainty, where the line between reality and the unknown would blur in ways he could never have imagined.

## The Time-Worn Messages

The next few days passed in a blur for Aditya Mehra. The vintage phone, now a constant companion, had become both a source of fascination and anxiety. Each day, a new message would appear on its small screen, cryptic and fragmented, hinting at the future while offering little in the way of concrete guidance.

It was a rainy afternoon when the phone buzzed to life once again. Aditya, who had taken to carrying the phone with him everywhere, pulled it from his backpack and squinted at the screen. The message read:

Phone Screen: "The choices you make will shape the outcome. Beware the crossroads on the 5th day."

Aditya's brow furrowed. The vague warning was unsettling. What crossroads? What choices? He had no idea what the "5th day" referred to. Trying to make sense of it, he made a mental note to keep track of significant events over the next few days.

The following morning, as he walked to school, Aditya couldn't shake the feeling of being watched. The phone buzzed again, but this time, the message was more detailed:

Phone Screen: "A secret meeting. A hidden agenda. Trust no one but yourself."

Aditya's curiosity was piqued. The message seemed to be hinting at something happening at school. He couldn't imagine who might have a hidden agenda or what kind of secret meeting was being referenced. Still, he decided to stay vigilant and pay close attention to any unusual behavior from his classmates or teachers.

At school, Aditya kept his eyes and ears open. He noticed a group of students huddled together in whispered conversation near the library. It seemed innocent enough, but Aditya couldn't help but feel a sense of unease. Was this the secret meeting mentioned in the message?

During lunch, he found himself seated next to Riya, a friend he hadn't spoken to much recently. She seemed unusually distracted, her eyes darting around the cafeteria.

Aditya: (tentatively) "Hey, Riya. Everything okay?"

Riya: (forcing a smile) "Oh, yeah. Just a lot on my mind. You know, school and stuff."

Aditya was about to press further when the phone buzzed again. He slipped it from his pocket, hoping for more clarity. The new message was unsettling:

Phone Screen: "The event is closer than you think. Prepare for the unexpected."

Aditya's heart raced. The messages were becoming more urgent, and the vague hints were starting to pile up. He couldn't ignore the feeling that something major was about to happen. He needed to be prepared.

As the days went by, the messages continued to arrive, each one offering fragmented clues that Aditya struggled to piece together. He began to notice small changes in his environment—an unusual increase in school gossip, a rise in tensions among students, and a general sense of unease in his community.

On the 5$^{th}$ day, the phone buzzed with a new message:

Phone Screen: "The crossroads are upon you. Choose wisely."

Aditya knew this was the day the messages had been leading up to. He felt a mounting sense of dread and anticipation. He had no idea what choices he would have to make or what crossroads awaited him, but he knew he had to stay alert.

The day unfolded with an air of tension. Aditya's usual routines felt different, like they were part of a larger, more significant narrative. As he navigated the day, he kept the phone close, ready for any new messages that might offer guidance.

As the school day drew to a close, Aditya found himself reflecting on the mysterious messages and the strange occurrences of the past few days. He was no closer to understanding the full scope of the crisis, but he was determined to uncover the truth. With the phone as his guide and his instincts as his compass, Aditya prepared himself for whatever lay ahead, knowing that the choices he made would have far-reaching consequences.

In the quiet of the evening, with the rain tapping softly against his window, Aditya felt a deep resolve. The phone had given him a glimpse of a future that was yet to be written, and he was ready to face the challenges that awaited him.

## The Ripple Effect

The days following the mysterious messages from the vintage phone were both confusing and intense for Aditya Mehra. Determined to navigate the cryptic warnings, he began making decisions he hoped would avert the impending crisis. However, the consequences of his choices seemed to create a ripple effect, altering his life and the lives of those around him in ways he hadn't anticipated.

It started with small changes. Aditya, acting on the phone's guidance, decided to join a school committee that aimed to address student concerns. He hoped that by being proactive, he could prevent some of the negativity he sensed brewing among his peers. But instead of uniting the student body, his involvement seemed to create more divisions. His friends, who had been supportive, grew distant, feeling that he was becoming too absorbed in the committee's work and neglecting their friendships.

One afternoon, Aditya was at the library working on a project when he noticed Riya, his once-close friend, and a few others huddled in a corner, whispering animatedly. When Aditya approached, Riya looked up, her eyes clouded with a mix of frustration and sadness.

Aditya: "Hey, Riya. What's going on?"

Riya: (hesitantly) "We're just talking about some changes around school. You've been so focused on the committee. It feels like you're not really present anymore."

Aditya's heart sank. He hadn't realized how his commitment to the committee had affected his friendships. It was disheartening to see that his efforts, which were intended to improve the school environment, had instead created tension.

The phone buzzed again that evening, displaying a new message:

Phone Screen: "Be mindful of the ripples you create. Every action has a consequence."

The message resonated with Aditya as he grappled with the unintended fallout from his choices. It became clear that even though his intentions were good, the outcomes were far from what he had hoped. The weight of responsibility began to feel heavier, and the burden of knowing that his actions could lead to both positive and negative outcomes was overwhelming.

The next day, Aditya's struggle continued. He had decided to reach out to his teachers, trying to address some of the issues that were being discussed among students. His goal was to improve communication between students and faculty, but his efforts seemed to stir up more trouble. Some teachers felt that Aditya was questioning their authority, while others viewed his actions as a form of rebellion.

Teacher: "Aditya, your intentions are appreciated, but your approach needs to be more collaborative. We value your input, but it's crucial to maintain respect and understanding."

Despite his best intentions, Aditya found himself caught in a web of misunderstandings and strained relationships. His attempts to make things better were backfiring, and he was left feeling isolated and uncertain.

As the days passed, Aditya noticed more changes. Events that had once seemed straightforward now appeared complex and fraught with unexpected consequences. Friendships grew more strained, school activities became more contentious, and Aditya struggled to maintain a sense of normalcy amidst the chaos.

The phone buzzed yet again, and Aditya, feeling both apprehensive and hopeful, glanced at the new message:

Phone Screen: "Balance your actions with empathy. True change comes from understanding, not just intent."

The message struck a chord with Aditya. He realized that while he had been focused on making the right choices, he hadn't fully considered how his actions impacted those around him. He needed to balance his intentions with empathy and understanding, recognizing that real change required more than just good intentions.

Determined to correct his course, Aditya set out to mend his strained relationships. He began by reaching out to his friends, apologizing for his unintentional neglect, and seeking their perspectives on how he could better support them. He also made an effort to approach his interactions with teachers and peers with greater sensitivity, striving to understand their viewpoints and collaborate more effectively.

Through these efforts, Aditya slowly began to see improvements. Friendships that had seemed fragile started to heal, and the atmosphere at school became more cooperative. The ripple effect of his choices began to show signs of positive change, even as he continued to navigate the complexities of his journey.

Aditya knew that the path ahead would be challenging, but he was learning valuable lessons about the interplay of intention, action, and empathy. The phone's messages had guided him to understand that while he couldn't always control the outcomes, he could strive to act with thoughtfulness and compassion, creating ripples of positive change in his world.

## The Clash of Choices

Aditya Mehra was caught in a whirlwind of conflicting emotions and relationships. As he tried to follow the phone's cryptic guidance, his well-meaning actions increasingly seemed to stir up discord. The clash between his intentions and the resulting consequences reached a boiling point, leaving him grappling with whether he could truly alter the future or if some events were destined to happen.

It all began when Aditya decided to confront the growing tensions at school head-on. He had received a message from the phone suggesting that addressing a particular issue with the school administration could prevent a major crisis. The problem was, he wasn't sure which issue the phone was referring to. His best guess was that it involved the recent conflicts between students and teachers, so he organized a meeting to address grievances.

Aditya: "I believe we need to have a more open dialogue between students and teachers. We're all working towards the same goal, but it seems like there's a lot of misunderstanding."

At first, the meeting seemed to be making headway. Teachers and students voiced their concerns, and Aditya felt a glimmer of hope that he was on the right track. However, as the discussions progressed, it became clear that his approach had inadvertently exacerbated the tensions. Some students felt that their concerns were being dismissed, while teachers felt that their authority was being undermined.

Teacher: "Aditya, I appreciate your enthusiasm, but this meeting feels more like a critique than a constructive dialogue. We need to find a way to work together, not just air grievances."

The confrontation left Aditya feeling disheartened. He had intended to bridge the gap but ended up widening it. His frustration grew as he faced similar reactions at home. His parents, who had initially been supportive of his efforts, were now worried about his increasing preoccupation with the phone's messages.

Mother: "Aditya, you're spending so much time on this phone and these projects. It's affecting your grades and our family time. What's really going on?"

Aditya tried to explain, but his parents were skeptical. They worried that his focus on the future, based on the phone's cryptic guidance, was causing him to lose sight of the present. The tension at home grew, and Aditya felt increasingly isolated.

In the midst of this turmoil, Aditya's friends became more distant. Riya, in particular, felt betrayed by his recent actions. She had always been his confidant, but now she was hurt by his perceived neglect.

Riya: "You've been so consumed by this phone and the need to fix things that you've pushed us aside. We're your friends, Aditya. We need you here, not just working on some mysterious problem."

Aditya struggled with the growing conflict. The phone's messages had once seemed like a beacon of hope, but now they felt like curse, leading him to question whether his efforts were futile. He began to wonder if the future was set in stone, if the choices he was making were merely delaying the inevitable.

As he wrestled with these doubts, he revisited the phone's earlier messages, searching for clarity. He realized that the messages had been guiding him to make choices, not to dictate a specific outcome. The future was not a predetermined path but a landscape shaped by actions and decisions.

Phone Screen: "The future is shaped by your choices. Balance your actions with your heart's true intentions. The path is yours to forge."

The message gave Aditya a moment of insight. He understood that while he could influence the future, he needed to make decisions that reflected his values and understanding, rather than reacting solely to the phone's guidance. He had to balance his desire to prevent a crisis with the need to remain true to himself and his relationships.

Aditya decided to approach his challenges differently. He began focusing on repairing his relationships and finding ways to address the issues he faced with a more balanced perspective. He worked to rebuild trust with his friends, sought a compromise with his parents, and approached his school projects with a more collaborative mindset

The journey was far from easy, but Aditya's efforts began to show signs of positive change. The tensions at school gradually eased, and his relationships started to heal. Although the future remained uncertain, Aditya was learning to navigate it with greater wisdom and resilience.

The clash of choices had taught Aditya an invaluable lesson: while he couldn't control every outcome, he could shape his journey by acting with integrity and understanding. The phone's messages continued to guide him, but he was now using them as tools for reflection rather than strict instructions. As Aditya embraced this new approach, he felt a renewed sense of hope and determination, ready to face whatever came next.

## The Hidden Truth

Aditya Mehra's journey with the mysterious phone had been a whirlwind of confusion and self-discovery.

Each message seemed to steer him through a maze of challenges, leaving him both hopeful and wary. As the tension from his recent choices began to settle, a new revelation emerged that would change his understanding of the phone and his place within his family's legacy.

It all began when Aditya was rummaging through some old family documents in the attic, trying to find clues about the phone's origins. Among the dusty papers and forgotten mementos, he stumbled upon a weathered journal belonging to his great-grandfather, Arvind Mehra. The journal's pages were filled with sketches, notes, and reflections that piqued Aditya's curiosity.

Aditya: "This has to be it. This journal might explain everything."

As he flipped through the pages, Aditya discovered detailed diagrams and descriptions of a strange device—an old, vintage phone remarkably similar to the one he had found. His great-grandfather's writings revealed a fascinating and unexpected truth.

Journal Entry: "The phone is not merely a tool for communication. It is a guide designed to assist future generations in navigating the complexities of life. Its messages are crafted to challenge and shape the character of its user."

Aditya's eyes widened. He had always seen the phone as an enigmatic artifact from the future, but now it was clear that its origins were deeply rooted in his family's past. The phone was a creation of Arvind Mehra, intended to offer guidance and wisdom to those who used it.

Journal Entry: "The messages you will receive are not just warnings. They are tests of your integrity, resilience, and understanding. They will challenge you to grow, make difficult choices, and learn important lessons about responsibility, friendship, and self-worth."

Aditya realized that the phone's cryptic messages were more than just instructions—they were designed to teach him valuable life lessons. Each choice he had faced was not merely about preventing a crisis but about developing qualities that would help him become a better person.

The revelation about the phone's true purpose shifted Aditya's perspective. He understood that the conflicts and challenges he had encountered were not just obstacles but opportunities for personal growth. The strained relationships, the mistakes, and the moments of doubt were all part of a larger lesson in navigating life's complexities.

Determined to honor his great-grandfather's intentions, Aditya began to approach his challenges with a new mindset. He focused on understanding the deeper meanings behind the phone's messages and applied the lessons he learned to his everyday life.

In his interactions with friends, he became more empathetic and open-minded. He worked to mend the rifts that had formed and found ways to communicate more effectively. He also took greater responsibility for his actions, realizing that each choice had consequences not just for himself but for those around him.

Aditya: "I've learned that it's not just about what I do but how I approach each situation. The phone's messages were never about dictating the future but guiding me towards becoming a better person."

As Aditya embraced the lessons from his great-grandfather's legacy, he began to see positive changes in his life. His relationships improved, and he felt more confident in handling the challenges he faced. The phone's messages continued to arrive, but now they felt like affirmations rather than cryptic warnings.

The hidden truth about the phone had illuminated a path for Aditya. He understood that while the future remained uncertain, his character and actions could shape his journey in meaningful ways. The phone was no longer a source of fear or confusion but a symbol of the enduring wisdom passed down through generations.

As Aditya continued his journey, he felt a renewed sense of purpose. He was committed to living in a way that honored his great-grandfather's legacy, using the lessons he had learned to navigate the complexities of life with integrity and compassion. The phone, now a cherished artifact of his family's history, served as a reminder of the timeless wisdom that guided him on his path of self-discovery.

## Embracing the Journey

The weight of the phone's revelations had finally settled on Aditya Mehra. With a clearer understanding of his great-grandfather's intentions, he felt a profound shift in his approach to life. The once-mystifying device had transformed from an eerie relic into a beacon of wisdom, illuminating a path toward personal growth and responsible decision-making.

Aditya stood in front of his mirror, the phone resting on his desk. Its screen, now a familiar presence, no longer held the same foreboding messages. Instead, he had begun to see it as a tool to reinforce the values he wanted to embody. No longer driven by fear of an uncertain future, Aditya was ready to embrace the journey ahead.

Aditya: "I've been given the chance to shape my own destiny. It's time to take control of my future, not just by reacting to messages, but by living out the lessons I've learned."

He started with his friendships, recognizing the strains that had formed over the past weeks. Aditya reached out to his friends, acknowledging his mistakes and expressing his genuine desire to mend the relationships. He organized a gathering to apologize and reconnect, emphasizing how much they meant to him.

Aditya: "I know I've let things get in the way of our friendship. I'm sorry for that. I value our bond and want to make things right."

The heartfelt apologies were met with understanding and forgiveness. His friends, seeing the sincerity in his words, welcomed him back with open arms. They appreciated his willingness to confront his mistakes and take responsibility, and the bonds of their friendship grew stronger.

In addition to repairing personal relationships, Aditya turned his attention to his community. He noticed various issues that needed attention—neighborhood clean-ups, fundraising events for local causes, and mentoring younger students. Inspired by his new perspective, he took the initiative to contribute in meaningful ways.

Aditya: "It's not just about fixing what's wrong in my life. It's about making a positive impact on those around me. Every small act of kindness can make a difference."

He organized a community clean-up drive, mobilizing his friends and neighbors to join him in improving their local environment. The project not only made a tangible difference in the neighborhood but also fostered a sense of unity and shared purpose.

In school, Aditya approached his studies with renewed enthusiasm. He set goals for himself, not based on the phone's cryptic messages, but on his personal aspirations and interests. He pursued his passions, joined clubs, and took on leadership roles, all while maintaining a balanced approach to his academic and personal life.

Aditya: "I've realized that while the future holds many uncertainties, I can shape it through my actions and choices today. I need to focus on what truly matters to me and work towards it with dedication."

As Aditya embraced his journey, he found that the lessons he had learned extended beyond the phone's guidance. The values of empathy, responsibility, and self-awareness became central to his daily life. His decisions were no longer driven by a fear of potential crises but by a genuine desire to live a life of integrity and purpose.

His family noticed the positive changes in him. They were proud of the young man he was becoming—someone who was not only reflective and thoughtful but also proactive and compassionate. Aditya's growth was evident, and he felt a deep sense of fulfillment.

Aditya's Father: "You've come a long way, Aditya. We're proud of how you've handled everything. It's clear that you're making thoughtful decisions and truly embracing your journey."

As he looked back on his experiences, Aditya understood that the future was not a rigid path set by fate but a canvas shaped by his values and choices. The phone had been a guide, but the real lessons came from within. He had learned to navigate life with a balanced perspective, understanding that while the future could be influenced, it was ultimately defined by the present.

Aditya's journey was far from over, but he faced it with a renewed sense of confidence and purpose. He knew that the road ahead would have its own set of challenges, but he was prepared to meet them with the wisdom he had gained. With the lessons from the past and the promise of the future, Aditya embraced the journey ahead, ready to shape his destiny with hope and determination.

## The Final Choice

The days leading up to the critical event were charged with tension for Aditya Mehra. The cryptic messages from the vintage phone had guided him through a labyrinth of decisions, each one shaping his journey. Now, with the pivotal moment at hand, Aditya faced one final message—a last piece of guidance that promised to influence the outcome of the impending crisis.

The message flickered on the phone's small screen, its words clear yet burdened with gravity:

> **"The choice you make now will shape not only your future but also the futures of those who depend on you. Trust the message, or trust your instincts."**

Aditya felt the weight of the message settle on his shoulders. The urgency of the situation was palpable, and the responsibility he bore was immense. It wasn't just about his own future but the impact of his decision on his friends, family, and community. The idea of strictly adhering to the message from his future self felt confining, while the thought of trusting his own instincts was both liberating and intimidating.

He took a moment to reflect on his journey. The lessons learned—about self-awareness, empathy, and responsibility—had become integral to his decision-making. He had seen how his actions affected those around him and had grown in ways he never imagined. Now, faced with a choice that would determine the course of the crisis, he wondered whether the final message could truly capture the complexity of his current situation.

Seeking clarity, Aditya gathered his closest friends and family. He shared his predicament, the message from the phone, and his own doubts about the best course of action. Their support and perspective provided him with the insight he needed.

**Aditya's Friend, Rahul**: "You've come a long way, Aditya. Maybe it's time to trust what you've learned and make the decision that feels right to you."

**Aditya's Mother**: "It's not just about following instructions. It's about using everything you've learned to make the best choice for everyone involved."

Their encouragement resonated deeply with Aditya. He realized that the final decision wasn't merely about following a directive but about applying the wisdom he had accumulated. The true test lay in making a choice that aligned with his values and understanding of the situation.

With renewed clarity, Aditya evaluated his options. He considered the potential outcomes, the impact on those he cared about, and listened to his inner voice. The choice was daunting, but he felt a profound sense of calm as he made his decision. He chose to trust his instincts and the lessons he had learned, believing that this approach would yield the best outcome.

As the critical event unfolded, Aditya's choice proved pivotal. The crisis was averted, and the resolution brought positive changes to the lives of those affected. Aditya's decision, guided by both his own wisdom and the support of his loved ones, demonstrated the strength of his growth and the value of self-trust.

The vintage phone, once a source of uncertainty, had become a symbol of his journey toward self-discovery. It had taught him invaluable lessons about leadership, responsibility, and the intricacies of making tough choices. With the crisis behind him, Aditya looked to the future with a renewed sense of purpose and confidence.

He understood that the path ahead would present its own set of challenges, but he felt equipped to face them with the insights and resilience he had gained. The future was not a fixed destination but a landscape shaped by the choices he made today. Aditya's journey had prepared him to navigate the complexities of life with wisdom and self-assurance.

* * * * *

# THE GLOBAL CLASSROOM

## Arrival

Priya sat nervously in the back seat of her host family's car, clutching her backpack tightly. Her thoughts raced as she gazed out of the window, taking in the unfamiliar surroundings. It was her first time leaving India, and while she had been filled with excitement in the days leading up to her departure, now that she was here, a wave of anxiety washed over her. The prospect of spending the next six months in a small American town both thrilled and terrified her.

As the car drove through Brooksville, Priya couldn't help but notice how different everything was from what she was used to in Mumbai. The town was picturesque, with its tree-lined streets, neat lawns, and charming brick buildings that looked like they belonged in a postcard. There were no crowded streets, no honking cars, no bustling markets. Instead, there was a quiet stillness that felt almost too perfect. It was beautiful, but it also made her feel incredibly far from home.

She thought of her family—her parents, who had been so supportive of her decision to study abroad, and her younger brother, who had teased her relentlessly about missing Indian food. They had all gathered at the airport to see her off, their smiles masking the sadness in their eyes. Priya had waved until she could no longer see them, and only then had she allowed herself to feel the full weight of what she was doing. She was embarking on an adventure, yes, but she was also leaving behind everything she knew and loved.

"Are you excited for school tomorrow?" asked Mrs. Johnson, her host mother, glancing at Priya in the rearview mirror. Mrs. Johnson had picked her up from the airport with a warm smile and a bouquet of flowers, a gesture that had touched Priya deeply.

Priya nodded, forcing a smile despite the lump forming in her throat. "Yes, very much."

Mrs. Johnson smiled warmly, clearly trying to put her at ease. "You'll love it here, Priya. Brooksville High is a great school, and I'm sure you'll make lots of friends. Everyone is really friendly, and they're all excited to meet you."

Priya appreciated her host mother's kindness, but she couldn't shake the nervousness gnawing at her. What if she didn't fit in? What if she couldn't understand the classes, or worse, what if no one wanted to be her friend? She had heard that American high schools could be intimidating, with their cliques and complicated social hierarchies. Would she be able to find her place in this new world?

As they pulled up to the Johnsons' cozy home, Priya's nerves eased a bit. The house was warm and inviting, a two-story structure with a porch that wrapped around the front. Flower beds lined the walkway, and a small garden with neatly trimmed bushes greeted them. It was so different from the apartment building she lived in back home, where the noise of the city was a constant companion. Here, everything was quiet and peaceful, almost too quiet for someone used to the perpetual motion of Mumbai.

Mrs. Johnson parked the car and turned to Priya with an encouraging smile. "Welcome home, Priya."

The words "home" struck a chord with Priya. Could this place really become her home for the next six months? She took a deep breath, reminding herself of all the reasons she had wanted to come here in the first place. This was her chance to experience a new culture, to learn, to grow. She had always been curious about the world beyond India, and now she had the opportunity to see it firsthand.

She stepped out of the car, her legs feeling slightly wobbly from the long journey. As she followed Mrs. Johnson up the steps and through the front door, Priya was greeted by the warmth of the house. The interior was just as cozy as the outside, with wooden floors, soft rugs, and family photos adorning the walls. A faint smell of cinnamon lingered in the air, making the house feel even more welcoming.

"I hope you like your room," Mrs. Johnson said as she led Priya upstairs. "We tried to make it as comfortable as possible for you."

Priya's room was at the end of the hallway. When Mrs. Johnson opened the door, Priya couldn't help but smile. The room was small but charming, with a bed covered in a quilt, a wooden desk by the window, and a bookshelf filled with books and knickknacks. A vase of fresh flowers sat on the nightstand, and the walls were painted a soft blue. It was clear that a lot of thought had gone into making the room feel like a home away from home.

Priya placed her backpack on the bed and turned to Mrs. Johnson. "It's perfect. Thank you so much."

"We're glad you like it," Mrs. Johnson said, her eyes twinkling. "If you need anything, don't hesitate to ask. We want you to feel as comfortable as possible."

After Mrs. Johnson left her to settle in, Priya sat on the bed, taking in her surroundings. She pulled out her phone and sent a quick message to her parents, letting them know that she had arrived safely. As she waited for their reply, she glanced out the window. The view was different from what she was used to—there were no skyscrapers, no bustling streets, just a quiet neighborhood with neatly kept houses and a few kids playing in a nearby yard.

That night, Priya joined the Johnsons for dinner. The meal was simple but delicious—roast chicken, mashed potatoes, and steamed vegetables. It was different from the spicy curries and chapatis she was used to, but she enjoyed it nonetheless. The conversation around the table was easy and light, with Mrs. Johnson and her husband, Mr. Johnson, asking Priya about her journey, her family, and her life in India. Priya found herself talking about

Mumbai, sharing stories about her school, her friends, and the vibrant culture she came from.

The Johnsons listened intently, asking questions and expressing genuine interest in her stories. Priya appreciated how welcoming they were, how they made her feel like she was already a part of their family. It eased some of the homesickness she had felt earlier, replacing it with a sense of comfort.

After dinner, Priya retired to her room, feeling a mix of emotions. She was still nervous about the days ahead, but she also felt a small spark of excitement. This was the beginning of a new chapter in her life, one that was full of unknowns but also full of possibilities. As she lay in bed that night, staring up at the ceiling, Priya made a promise to herself: she would make the most of this experience. She would be open to new things, new people, and new challenges. She would embrace this adventure, no matter how difficult it might be at times.

And with that thought, Priya drifted off to sleep, dreaming of the new world she was about to discover.

## First Day

The next morning, Priya found herself standing in front of Brooksville High School, her heart pounding in her chest. The building was much larger than her school back in Mumbai, its red-brick exterior stretching high above her. The American flag fluttered in the morning breeze, and students milled around the entrance, chatting and laughing as they prepared for the day ahead. Priya took a deep breath, clutching the straps of her backpack. This was it—her first day in an American high school.

She wasn't alone in her anxiety, though. As she stepped inside, the hallway buzzed with energy, and Priya noticed a few other students who looked just as nervous as she felt. One was a tall boy with curly hair, wearing a soccer jersey from Brazil. His eyes darted around, taking in the unfamiliar surroundings. Another was a girl with a hijab, quietly adjusting her backpack as she stood near the lockers, her expression one of both curiosity and apprehension.

Priya caught their eyes and offered a small, encouraging smile. They exchanged brief nods, a silent acknowledgment of the shared experience of being new in a strange place. It was comforting to know that she wasn't the only one feeling out of place.

As they were introduced to their new classmates, Priya quickly realized that cultural differences weren't just about language. The teachers and students spoke quickly, their American accents unfamiliar and, at times, hard to understand. During her first class, Priya found herself struggling to keep up with the fast-paced English, her mind racing to translate words and phrases that were unfamiliar to her. Back in Mumbai, she had been confident in her English skills, but here, in the middle of a lively discussion, she felt out of her depth.

She also noticed that some students seemed hesitant to talk to her. While many were friendly and welcoming, others kept their distance, unsure of how to approach someone from a different background. Priya wondered if they were curious about her but didn't know what to say, or if they simply didn't know how to relate to someone who had grown up so far away. The thought made her feel more isolated, as if there was an invisible barrier between her and her new classmates.

Despite these initial challenges, Priya was determined to make the most of her experience. She reminded herself that she was here to learn and grow, not just academically, but personally as well. She was particularly curious about the other exchange students, who seemed to be navigating similar struggles. During lunch, she spotted the boy with the soccer jersey and the girl with the hijab sitting at a table near the window. Taking a deep breath, she decided to join them, hoping to find some common ground.

"Hi, I'm Priya," she introduced herself with a friendly smile as she approached the table.

The boy with the soccer jersey grinned back, his dark eyes lighting up. "I'm Thiago, from Brazil," he said, his accent rich and musical. His confidence was evident, though Priya could sense that he, too, was feeling the weight of being in a new environment.

The girl in the hijab nodded politely. "I'm Amira, from Egypt," she said, her voice soft but steady. There was a quiet strength in her eyes, and Priya could tell that Amira was someone who carried herself with dignity, even in the face of uncertainty.

Sitting beside them was a girl with long dark hair and a serious expression. "I'm Mei, from China," she introduced herself, her voice measured and calm. Mei seemed more reserved than the others, but there was a quiet determination in her demeanor that Priya found intriguing.

As they began to share their stories, Priya felt a sense of relief. Each of them had their own unique challenges and experiences, but they were all going through the same adjustments. Thiago talked about how different everything was from his life in São Paulo, where soccer was a way of life and the city buzzed with energy at all hours. Amira shared her experience of balancing her faith with the new culture, and the small but significant challenges she faced, like finding a quiet place to pray during school hours. Mei spoke about the differences in education systems, how she missed the discipline and structure of her school back in Beijing.

Priya found herself opening up about her own experiences, the homesickness that lingered in her heart, and the difficulty of adjusting to the fast-paced English spoken here. She talked about Mumbai, the city she loved, with its vibrant chaos, the smell of street food, and the sound of honking cars at all hours. Her new friends listened intently, nodding in understanding. They, too, missed their homes, and it was comforting to share those feelings with people who understood.

As the lunch period went on, the conversation shifted from their struggles to their hopes for the future. They bonded over their love of home, their excitement about being in a new country, and their determination to make the most of this opportunity. Priya felt a warm sense of connection with Thiago, Amira, and Mei. They were from different parts of the world, but here, in this small American town, they were united by their shared experience.

By the time lunch ended, Priya no longer felt quite so alone. She had found friends who understood her journey, and that gave her the strength to face the challenges ahead. As they left the cafeteria together, laughing about something Thiago had said, Priya felt a flicker of hope. This new world was daunting, but with friends like these, she knew she could navigate it.

## Cultural Clashes

As the weeks went by, the exchange students began to settle into their new lives at Brooksville High. The initial excitement of being in a new country started to give way to the realities of adjusting to a different culture. The novelty of their surroundings was still there, but so were the challenges that came with being strangers in a strange land. With every passing day, they grew more familiar with their new routines, but they also encountered cultural clashes that tested their patience and resilience.

For Priya, these clashes often manifested in the form of well-meaning but misguided questions from her classmates. One day, during a history class discussion about colonialism, a student turned to her and asked, "So, do you speak Indian?" The question was innocent enough, but it left Priya feeling a mix of frustration and sadness. She had grown up in a country with a rich tapestry of languages, each one with its own history and significance. Yet here she was, being asked about "Indian" as if it were a single language.

"Actually, India has over a thousand languages," Priya explained, trying to hide her irritation. "I speak Hindi and

Marathi, but there are many other languages spoken across the country." She wanted to add that even within a single state, multiple languages and dialects coexisted, but she wasn't sure her classmate would fully understand.

The student blinked in surprise. "Wow, I had no idea," they admitted, looking a bit embarrassed. Priya could see that they were genuinely interested in learning more, but the encounter left her feeling isolated. It was a reminder that, despite being surrounded by people, she was still very much alone in her experience as an Indian in a predominantly white American town.

Thiago, too, faced his share of cultural misunderstandings. During gym class, the topic of sports inevitably came up, and one of the boys eagerly asked him, "So, you must be amazing at soccer, right? I mean, you're from Brazil!"

Thiago smiled, but there was a hint of frustration behind it. "I do play soccer, but not everyone in Brazil does," he explained. "There are lots of other sports and activities people are into back home. We're not just about soccer."

But the assumptions didn't stop there. Thiago found himself constantly explaining that Brazil was more than just a land of beaches, Carnival, and soccer. He talked about the diversity of his country, from the Amazon rainforest to the bustling cities, and how different regions had their own distinct cultures and traditions. Yet, he couldn't help but feel that his peers saw him as a representative of all things Brazilian, rather than as an individual with his own unique experiences and interests.

Amira's challenges were different but equally difficult. As one of the few Muslim students at Brooksville High, she often found herself having to explain her faith to curious classmates. While some asked thoughtful questions, others made assumptions that were hurtful, even if unintentionally so. One day, during lunch, a girl approached Amira and hesitantly asked, "Do you have to wear that scarf all the time? Like, even at home?"

Amira took a deep breath before responding. "No, I don't have to wear it at home, and I don't have to wear it at all if I don't want to," she said calmly. "But I choose to wear it because it's an important part of my identity and faith. It's something that makes me feel closer to God and reminds me of my values."

The girl nodded, seemingly satisfied with the answer, but Amira couldn't shake the feeling of being under a microscope. She knew that her classmates were simply curious, but the constant need to explain herself was exhausting. She longed for the day when her hijab would be seen not as a symbol of otherness, but as just another part of who she was.

Mei, on the other hand, found herself struggling with the cultural differences in how people communicated and interacted. In China, she had been taught to be quiet, respectful, and to avoid drawing attention to herself. But here, in the United States, she found that her reserved nature was often misunderstood. Teachers encouraged her to speak up more in class, to participate in discussions and share her opinions. Some of her classmates even assumed she was uninterested or aloof because she wasn't as outgoing as they were.

One day, after a particularly frustrating group project where her ideas were overlooked, Mei confided in Priya. "I just don't understand why everyone here is so loud," she said, her voice tinged with frustration. "Back home, we're taught to listen more than we speak, to think carefully before we say anything. But here, it feels like if you don't speak up right away, you're ignored."

Priya nodded sympathetically. "It's the same for me," she admitted. "In India, we respect our elders and teachers by listening quietly, but here, it's like everyone's expected to have an opinion on everything all the time. It's exhausting."

Despite these challenges, the exchange students found solace in each other's company. They had become a tight-knit group, bonded by their shared experiences of navigating a new culture. Whenever one of them faced a difficult situation, the others were there to offer support, advice, and a listening ear. They spent hours together after school, talking about their frustrations, their homesickness, and their hopes for the future. These conversations became a lifeline, helping them to process their emotions and find strength in their shared journey.

One day, during lunch, Priya brought up an idea that had been on her mind for a while. "What if we organized a cultural showcase?" she suggested, her eyes lighting up with excitement. "We could present food, music, and traditions from our home countries. It could be a way to educate our classmates and break down some of the stereotypes we've been dealing with."

Thiago's face lit up at the idea. "I love that! I could do a capoeira demonstration and show everyone some Brazilian moves."

Amira nodded thoughtfully. "I could bring some traditional Egyptian dishes, and maybe do a henna demonstration. It would be a great way to share our culture with everyone."

Mei, who had been listening quietly, smiled softly. "I could show some Chinese calligraphy and maybe demonstrate a traditional tea ceremony. It would be nice to share a part of my culture with the school."

With their plan in motion, the exchange students approached the school administration, who were enthusiastic about the idea. They were given the green light to organize the event, and soon the entire school was buzzing with anticipation. Over the next few weeks, Priya, Thiago, Amira, and Mei poured their hearts into preparing for the cultural showcase. They spent countless hours cooking, practicing performances, and creating displays that represented the essence of their home countries.

The day of the showcase finally arrived, and the school gymnasium was transformed into a vibrant celebration of cultures. Tables were set up with dishes from India, Brazil, Egypt, and China, each one a feast for the senses. The air was filled with the tantalizing aromas of spices, freshly baked bread, and sweet desserts. Students and teachers wandered from table to table, sampling the food, listening to traditional music, and learning about the different customs and traditions.

Priya felt a swell of pride as she watched her classmates try the spicy samosas and sweet jalebis she had made. Their eyes widened in surprise at the burst of flavors, and they asked her questions about the ingredients and the cultural significance of the dishes. It was a chance for Priya to share a piece of her home with them, and she relished the opportunity to teach them about the diversity of Indian cuisine.

Thiago's capoeira demonstration drew a crowd, with students eagerly trying to mimic his graceful, acrobatic moves. He explained the history of capoeira, how it had originated as a form of resistance among enslaved Africans in Brazil, and how it had evolved into a popular martial art and dance. As he taught his peers the basic steps, Thiago felt a sense of connection with them, a bridge between his world and theirs.

Amira's henna station was a hit, with students lining up to have intricate designs drawn on their hands. As she worked, she explained the cultural significance of henna in Egypt, how it was used in celebrations and ceremonies, and the meaning behind the patterns she created. For Amira, it was a chance to show her peers that her culture was rich, vibrant, and full of beauty.

Mei's calligraphy and tea ceremony captivated her classmates, who watched in awe as she demonstrated the delicate art of writing Chinese characters with a brush. She explained the philosophy behind the tea ceremony, how it was a form of meditation and a way to cultivate harmony and respect. For Mei, it was a way to share the quiet, introspective side of her culture, something that was often overlooked in the fast-paced environment of an American high school.

As the day went on, the cultural showcase became more than just an event; it became a celebration of diversity, a space where differences were not just acknowledged, but embraced. The exchange students had not only shared their cultures with their peers, but they had also learned more about themselves in the process. They had faced challenges, but they had also found strength in their identities, in the richness of their heritage, and in the bonds they had formed with each other.

By the time the event ended, Priya, Thiago, Amira, and Mei were exhausted but deeply satisfied. They had successfully shared a piece of their home with their new community, and in doing so, they had made Brooksville High a little more inclusive, a little more understanding. As they packed up their displays and

said goodbye to their classmates, Priya felt a sense of accomplishment. She knew there would still be challenges ahead, but she also knew that she wasn't alone. She had friends who understood her journey, and a school that was now a little more open to the world.

## Building Bridges

The success of the cultural showcase reverberated through the halls of Brooksville High School. What began as a simple idea to share their heritage had blossomed into an event that touched the lives of everyone involved. For Priya and her friends, it was a moment of triumph, where the fears and uncertainties that had plagued them since their arrival seemed to melt away in the warmth of newfound connections.

The next morning, Priya walked into school with a lightness in her step. The previous evening had left her exhilarated, and she noticed the difference immediately.

The usual whispers and sideways glances were replaced by smiles and greetings. Students who had once seemed distant now waved to her in the hallway, some even stopping to chat.

"Priya! I loved the Bollywood dance last night!" a girl from her math class called out as she passed. "You have to teach me more moves!"

Priya grinned, the memory of the dance session flooding back. She had been nervous at first, worried that her classmates might find the music too foreign or the steps too difficult. But as the room filled with the upbeat rhythms of a popular Bollywood song, she saw their faces light up with excitement. They followed her lead with enthusiasm, laughing as they stumbled through the moves but never losing their joy.

The transformation in her peers was striking. Where there had once been hesitation and curiosity tinged with doubt, there was now genuine interest and admiration. Priya had always taken pride in her culture, but seeing it embraced by others in this way was a new and exhilarating experience.

Thiago, too, basked in the afterglow of the event. The soccer match he organized had drawn students from all corners of the school. Whether they were experienced players or complete novices, everyone seemed eager to join in. The game had quickly turned into a lively, chaotic affair, with laughter and shouts echoing across the field.

As the match progressed, Thiago found himself in the center of it all, effortlessly weaving through players, passing the ball, and encouraging others to get involved.

For a brief moment, the soccer field became a microcosm of the world, where differences in language, culture, and background were irrelevant. All that mattered was the shared love of the game.

Afterward, students who had never spoken to him before came up to congratulate him, expressing their admiration for his skills and thanking him for organizing such a fun activity. For Thiago, the match was more than just a game—it was a symbol of how sports could bridge cultural divides and bring people together in ways that words sometimes couldn't.

Amira, on the other hand, found herself surrounded by a curious crowd at her station, eager to learn more about her culture and religion. Throughout the evening, she explained the significance of Ramadan and why she wore a hijab. As she handed out the traditional Egyptian sweets she had prepared, her classmates asked thoughtful questions, showing a level of respect and understanding that Amira hadn't expected.

She had worried that her peers would see her as different, maybe even too different to relate to. But as she spoke about the traditions she cherished, Amira realized that her classmates weren't just interested—they were genuinely eager to learn. One student even asked if they could try fasting for a day to understand what it felt like, a gesture that touched Amira deeply.

The cultural showcase allowed Amira to share a part of herself that she had often kept hidden. And in doing so, she discovered that the differences that once seemed like barriers could actually be the foundation for new connections. By opening up about her experiences, she found common ground with students she had never imagined would understand her journey.

Mei, the quietest of the group, had been apprehensive about her role in the showcase. She had always been more comfortable observing from the sidelines rather than being the center of attention. But as students lined up to learn Chinese calligraphy, Mei's nerves slowly faded.

With careful precision, she demonstrated how to hold the brush, how to angle it just right, and how to let the ink flow onto the paper in deliberate, graceful strokes. Her classmates watched in awe as she wrote their names in Chinese characters, each one a small masterpiece in itself.

Mei had always loved the art of calligraphy, but seeing her peers' fascination with it was a new experience. They marveled at the complexity of the characters and the beauty of the script, asking Mei to explain the meaning behind each stroke. As she patiently guided them through the process, Mei felt a sense of pride swelling in her chest. This was her culture, her heritage, and it was being celebrated in a way she had never expected.

As the night drew to a close, the exchange students found themselves gathered in a quiet corner of the gymnasium, watching the scene unfold before them. The room buzzed with conversation and laughter as students mingled, tasted new foods, and tried out dance moves and calligraphy techniques. The cultural showcase had done more than just educate—it had transformed the school, creating an atmosphere of openness and curiosity that had been missing before.

"Can you believe how well this went?" Priya whispered, her voice tinged with disbelief and pride.

Thiago nodded, a satisfied smile on his face. "I think we did something really special here. Look at them—they're not just asking about our cultures; they're trying to understand us as people."

Amira, who had been quietly observing the scene, spoke up. "I was so worried about standing out too much, but now I see that sharing who we are is what makes us stronger. We've shown them that there's more to us than just being 'the exchange students.' We're part of this community now."

Mei, always thoughtful, added, "It's amazing how something as simple as sharing our traditions can change the way people see us. I feel like they finally see me, not just as the girl from China, but as someone with a rich culture and a story to tell."

The four exchange students had come to Brooksville as strangers, each carrying their own fears and insecurities. But through the cultural showcase, they had found their place in the school. The event had been more than just a display of their heritage—it was a bridge, connecting them to their peers in ways they hadn't anticipated.

As they left the gymnasium, the exchange students walked together, a sense of camaraderie and accomplishment filling the air. They knew that the journey ahead would still have its challenges, but they also knew that they had each other to rely on. They had built bridges, not just with their classmates, but with one another, and those bridges would carry them through whatever came next.

In the days and weeks that followed, the impact of the cultural showcase continued to be felt throughout Brooksville High. Students who had previously kept to themselves began reaching out, forming new friendships that crossed cultural boundaries. The school, once divided by cliques and misunderstandings, was slowly becoming a more inclusive and welcoming place.

Priya, Thiago, Amira, and Mei were no longer just the exchange students—they were valued members of the Brooksville community, each bringing their own unique perspective and enriching the lives of those around them. The cultural showcase had been a turning point, a moment when they realized that their differences were not something to hide but something to celebrate.

As Priya walked home that evening, she couldn't help but feel a deep sense of peace. She was far from home, but in Brooksville, she had found a new one. And with her friends by her side, she knew that anything was possible. The future was bright, full of promise and potential, and Priya was ready to embrace it with open arms.

## Lessons Learned

As the final weeks of their exchange program in Brooksville drew to a close, Priya, Thiago, Amira, and Mei found themselves reflecting on the whirlwind of experiences that had shaped their time in the small American town. What had started as an intimidating adventure into the unknown had transformed into a journey of self-discovery, growth, and the forging of unbreakable bonds.

For Priya, the shy girl who had once sat nervously in the back seat of her host family's car, clutching her backpack tightly, the transformation was profound. When she first arrived, she worried about how she would fit in, fearing that her Indian heritage might set her apart too much. But over time, those fears faded as she embraced who she was and shared her culture with her new friends. The Bollywood dance she had taught at the cultural showcase was now a favorite memory among her classmates, who often asked her to teach them more moves.

More importantly, Priya had learned to take pride in her heritage in a way she hadn't before. Her time in Brooksville had shown her that being different wasn't something to be ashamed of—it was something to be celebrated. She had grown from a girl anxious about fitting in to a confident young woman who understood that her culture was an integral part of her identity, something she could share proudly with the world.

Thiago, the exuberant Brazilian boy who had first bonded with his classmates over soccer, had also undergone a significant transformation. While soccer remained a passion, Thiago realized that it wasn't the only thing that defined him. His experiences in Brooksville taught him that he was more than just an athlete; he was also a friend, a leader, and someone who could bridge cultural gaps with humor, kindness, and understanding. The soccer match he organized during the cultural showcase had been a highlight, but it was the friendships he formed off the field that left the deepest impression on him.

Thiago had always been outgoing, but his time in Brooksville helped him discover new facets of his personality. He learned to listen more, to be patient, and to appreciate the quiet moments as much as the exciting ones. He returned home with a broader perspective on the world, carrying with him the knowledge that his identity was multi-faceted and that his cultural background was just one of the many aspects that made him who he was.

Amira's journey had been one of balance and self-acceptance. When she first arrived in Brooksville, she worried that her faith and cultural practices would set her apart. The hijab she wore and her observance of Ramadan initially made her feel like she was walking on a tightrope between her beliefs and her new surroundings. But as the weeks went by, Amira found a way to harmonize her faith with her life in Brooksville.

The cultural showcase had been a turning point for her. The opportunity to share the significance of Ramadan and the meaning behind her hijab with her classmates not only educated them but also empowered her. Amira realized that she didn't have to choose between her faith and her new life—she could embrace both. The support and understanding from her friends and classmates gave her the confidence to be herself, fully and unapologetically.

By the end of the program, Amira had become a role model for others, showing that it was possible to stay true to your beliefs while also being open to new experiences. She returned to Egypt with a newfound sense of confidence and a deeper appreciation for the strength of her convictions.

Mei, who had started her journey as the quiet and reserved student from China, experienced a transformation that surprised even herself. Initially, her shyness made it difficult for her to connect with others, and she often found herself retreating into the comfort of familiar routines. But Brooksville had a way of drawing her out of her shell. The cultural showcase, where she shared the art of Chinese calligraphy, was a turning point.

Through the careful strokes of her brush, Mei not only introduced her classmates to the beauty of her culture but also discovered her own strength. She realized that her shyness didn't have to be a barrier—it could be a strength. Mei's quiet determination and her ability to listen deeply made her a valued friend and confidante. Her classmates began to seek her out, not just for her calligraphy skills, but for her thoughtful insights and her calm, steady presence.

As the program came to an end, Mei felt a sense of accomplishment. She had learned to embrace both her shyness and her strengths, understanding that they were both integral parts of who she was. She returned to China with a new sense of self-assurance and the knowledge that she could make a difference in the world, even in her own quiet way.

As the day of their departure approached, the exchange students found themselves standing at the Brooksville High School gates, the place that had become so much more than just a school to them. It was here that they had faced their fears, embraced their differences, and forged friendships that transcended borders.

"I can't believe it's time to go," Priya said, her voice tinged with sadness and gratitude. "It feels like we just got here, but at the same time, I feel like I've grown so much."

Thiago nodded, his usual smile a little softer. "Yeah, it's strange. We're going back home, but we're not the same people we were when we arrived."

Amira looked around at the familiar surroundings, a sense of peace settling over her. "We've learned so much here—about ourselves, about each other, and about the world. I think that's something we'll carry with us forever."

Mei, who had been quiet, finally spoke. "I'll miss this place, but I'm also excited to take everything I've learned back home. We've all changed, and I think that's a good thing."

As they prepared to leave Brooksville, the exchange students knew that the experiences they had shared and the lessons they had learned would stay with them for the rest of their lives. They had navigated cultural differences, faced challenges, and come out stronger on the other side. More importantly, they had made friendships that would last a lifetime, friendships that had shown them the power of acceptance, empathy, and understanding.

Brooksville, too, had been changed by their presence. The small town, once somewhat insular and unaware of the richness of global cultures, had been opened up by the exchange students' stories, experiences, and willingness to share their lives. The cultural showcase had been just the beginning; the conversations and connections that followed had left an indelible mark on the community. The students and teachers alike had learned that diversity was not something to be feared but something to be celebrated.

As the four friends said their goodbyes, they knew that this was not the end, but rather the beginning of a new chapter in their lives. They had learned that cultural differences, while sometimes challenging, were also what made life rich and interesting. They had learned that acceptance, empathy, and friendship could bridge any gap and that these values had not only helped them navigate their time in a new country but had also made them better people.

As they boarded the plane, each of them looked out at the town that had become a second home. They were leaving Brooksville, but they were taking a piece of it with them. And in turn, they were leaving behind a piece of themselves—a legacy of understanding, connection, and the realization that, despite our differences, we are all more alike than we think.

* * * * *

# GHOSTS OF SUMMER

## Arrival

The summer sun cast a warm golden hue over the landscape as Priya, Aarav, Kavya, and Rohan approached the old family estate. Priya's heart fluttered with a mix of anticipation and anxiety. The mansion, nestled amidst dense woods and sprawling meadows, looked both majestic and forlorn, its once-proud façade now weathered by time. The wrought-iron gate, adorned with intricate but rusting patterns, creaked open to reveal a driveway lined with overgrown weeds and tangled ivy.

Priya glanced back at her friends, each of whom had varying degrees of excitement and apprehension. Aarav, with his usual air of skepticism, was already scrutinizing the mansion with a wary eye. "This place is massive. I didn't expect it to be so... gothic," he remarked, adjusting the strap of his backpack.

Kavya, ever the dreamer, gazed at the mansion with wide eyes, her imagination already running wild. "It's like something out of a classic novel," she mused, reaching out to touch the cold iron gate. "I bet it has a ton of stories waiting to be discovered."

Rohan, practical and grounded, was focused on the logistics. "Looks like we'll need a serious cleanup," he said, surveying the debris and dust. "Let's get our stuff inside before it gets dark."

The group moved their bags from the station wagon into the grand entrance hall of the mansion. The front door, once polished wood, now had a layer of grime and cobwebs. Priya fumbled with the ancient brass key, the weight of the keyring clinking as she unlocked the door. It swung open with a reluctant groan, revealing a dimly lit foyer.

Inside, the mansion was a relic of a bygone era. The high ceilings were adorned with faded frescoes, and the walls were lined with portraits of stern-faced ancestors whose eyes seemed to follow them with a disquieting intensity. Dust motes floated lazily in the shafts of light streaming through the dirty, cracked windows. The grand staircase, with its ornate wooden banister, ascended into shadowy upper floors, its steps creaking ominously underfoot.

"Wow, this place is... something else," Aarav said, his voice echoing slightly in the cavernous space. "It's like stepping into another time."

They began their exploration, each room revealing its own unique character. The library, with its towering shelves of ancient, leather-bound books, was filled with a musty odor and a thick layer of dust. The massive fireplace in the living room was cold and empty, its hearth filled with ashes and cobwebs. Priya's excitement was tempered by a growing sense of unease as the house seemed to respond to their presence with subtle, unsettling phenomena.

As they made their way through the rooms, Priya felt a chill that had nothing to do with the temperature. The air seemed to grow colder with each step, and she noticed the shadows in the corners of the rooms appeared unusually deep and restless. The mansion, though still and silent, felt as though it was holding its breath, waiting for something.

During their exploration, Kavya stumbled upon an old, ornate mirror leaning against a dusty wall. "Look at this," she called out, her voice filled with awe. The mirror's frame was intricately carved with floral patterns, but the glass was cloudy and cracked. As Kavya reached out to brush off the dust, a sudden cold draft swept through the room, making the candle flames flicker erratically.

"What was that?" Rohan asked, glancing around warily. The temperature in the room had dropped noticeably, and the group huddled closer together, trying to shake off the eerie feeling.

"I think it's just the old windows," Priya suggested, though her voice lacked conviction. She could feel her heartbeat quicken as the house seemed to come alive with an unsettling energy.

The group continued to explore, eventually making their way to the kitchen. The space was cluttered with outdated appliances and grimy countertops. They attempted to make a simple meal, but the eerie feeling persisted. Every creak of the floorboards and every whisper of the wind outside seemed amplified in the oppressive silence of the mansion.

As evening descended, the once-welcoming mansion took on a more foreboding character. The setting sun cast long, distorted shadows across the walls, and the cold draft that had begun earlier grew stronger. The friends gathered in the dining room, a cavernous space with a grand wooden table set for their first meal. The large chandelier above them, covered in dust, seemed to sway slightly as if disturbed by an unseen hand.

The conversation during dinner was strained, each member of the group trying to ignore the unsettling sensations that had begun to invade their senses. The silence was occasionally broken by the creaking of the house and the distant sound of something heavy being dragged across the floor. Priya tried to reassure her friends, but her own nerves were on edge.

Just as they began to relax, a loud crash echoed through the mansion. The sound came from the upper floors, and it was followed by a moment of eerie silence. The friends exchanged anxious glances, their earlier bravado giving way to palpable fear.

"We should check that out," Priya suggested, trying to sound braver than she felt.

They climbed the grand staircase, the steps groaning under their weight. The upper floor was cloaked in darkness, and the narrow hallway seemed to stretch endlessly. The cold draft was more pronounced here, and each gust felt like an icy hand brushing against their skin.

At the end of the hall, they discovered the source of the crash: a large, ornate mirror had fallen from its place on the wall and shattered into a thousand pieces on the floor. The room was filled with the sharp, metallic smell of broken glass.

"Seems like the mirror just fell," Aarav said, kneeling to examine the shards. "But why would it fall like that?"

Rohan noticed a cold spot near the window and remarked, "It's freezing here. Maybe the house is just drafty."

As they cleaned up the broken glass, the whispers they had earlier dismissed as the wind now seemed to grow louder and more distinct. The shadows in the corners of the rooms seemed to shift and pulse with an unnatural rhythm.

By the time they retired to their rooms, the mansion felt different—more alive, more aware. Each creak of the floorboards and each whisper of the wind seemed to carry a hidden message. As they lay in their beds, the oppressive silence of the mansion pressed down on them, making sleep difficult. The friends could not shake the feeling that the house had secrets—secrets that were beginning to awaken.

The night stretched on, and the mansion's shadows seemed to deepen, wrapping around Priya, Aarav, Kavya, and Rohan like a dark, heavy cloak. Unseen eyes seemed to watch their every move, and the echoes of the past began to stir, preparing to reveal themselves.

## First Encounter

The morning sun struggled to penetrate the grime-coated windows of the mansion, casting feeble rays that barely reached the dusty floors. Priya, Aarav, Kavya, and Rohan gathered for breakfast in the cavernous dining room, where the shadows seemed to cling to the corners, never fully dissipating. The cold, muted light did little to lift their spirits.

Priya, feeling the weight of last night's unsettling atmosphere, hesitated over her cereal. The group's conversation was stilted, each member lost in their thoughts about the strange occurrences. Aarav's skepticism was evident as he poked at his food, while Kavya's eyes wandered around the room, searching for anything out of place. Rohan, the most pragmatic, was focused on the task at hand, trying to keep the group's morale up.

"I didn't sleep well," Priya admitted, her voice barely above a whisper. "Did anyone else feel something strange last night?"

Kavya nodded vigorously. "I felt it too. It was like the house was alive, almost as if it was breathing."

Rohan cleared his throat, trying to sound reassuring. "It's an old house. Old houses creak and groan. We probably just need to get used to it."

Aarav, ever the skeptic, shrugged. "Well, if you're so convinced, let's find out what's going on. Maybe there's a logical explanation for all these strange feelings."

The group decided to split up for a more thorough exploration of the mansion. Priya and Kavya headed to the library, a room that had intrigued them from the start. The library's grand entrance was flanked by towering shelves lined with faded, leather-bound books.

The air was thick with the musty scent of aged paper, and the dim light filtering through the grimy windows created a somber ambiance.

As Priya and Kavya began to explore, they noticed the library's ornate fireplace, its mantel cluttered with dusty trinkets and forgotten relics. Priya's attention was drawn to a small, ornate wooden box partially hidden behind a stack of old books. The box's intricate carvings depicted scenes of pastoral life, and it seemed oddly out of place among the dust-covered volumes.

"What do you think this is?" Priya asked, her curiosity piqued.

Kavya's eyes widened as she carefully brushed away the thick layer of dust. "It looks like a keepsake box. Let's see what's inside."

Priya opened the box with a soft creak. Inside lay an old, leather-bound journal. The cover was faded and cracked, but the pages inside appeared surprisingly well-preserved. Kavya's fingers trembled slightly as she opened the journal, revealing handwritten entries that chronicled the life of Eleanor, a former resident of the mansion.

The entries were filled with cryptic and haunting descriptions. Eleanor wrote about "whispers in the dark," "shadowy figures that flitted past the windows," and a "troubled spirit" that seemed to haunt the estate. The language was evocative and eerie, hinting at a deep sadness and unresolved conflicts. Priya and Kavya read through the pages, absorbing the chilling accounts of strange occurrences and growing unrest.

"This is incredible," Kavya said, her voice barely above a whisper. "It's like Eleanor was experiencing the same things we are."

Priya nodded, feeling a shiver run down her spine. "We need to find out more about Eleanor and her family. There might be clues here about why the house is haunted."

As they delved deeper into the journal, Priya felt a sudden, sharp chill. The temperature in the room seemed to drop precipitously, and a cold draft swept through the library. Priya looked up, her breath catching in her throat. There, in the corner of the room, a faint, ghostly figure began to materialize.

The figure was that of a young girl, no older than twelve, with dark, sorrowful eyes and an expression of fear. Her translucent form shimmered in the dim light, and her presence was both fragile and unsettling. She wore a simple, old-fashioned dress that looked out of place in the modern world.

"Help me," the ghostly girl whispered, her voice barely audible above the eerie silence. Her eyes were filled with a desperate longing as she extended a trembling hand toward Priya.

Priya's heart raced as she took a tentative step forward. "Wait—" she began, but the ghost vanished before she could reach her. The room grew cold and still, the temperature plummeting even further. Priya stood frozen, her mind reeling from the encounter.

Kavya, who had been observing in wide-eyed silence, finally found her voice. "What just happened? Did you see that?"

Priya nodded, her voice shaking. "Yes, I saw her. She looked so scared. She said, 'Help me,' and then she disappeared."

Kavya's face was pale, her hands clutching the journal tightly. "We need to tell the others. They might have experienced something similar or found more clues."

The two friends hurried to find Aarav and Rohan. They found them exploring the upper floors, examining old photographs and dusty relics. Priya and Kavya relayed their encounter and showed them the journal.

"That's unbelievable," Aarav said, his skepticism momentarily set aside. "If Eleanor was documenting these occurrences, there might be more to discover."

Rohan nodded in agreement. "Let's gather all the information we can. We need to understand the history of this place and the people who lived here."

The group reconvened in the library, poring over the journal and other documents they had found. They discovered more letters and personal effects hidden away in drawers and behind loose panels. Each piece of evidence offered a glimpse into the mansion's troubled past, hinting at a legacy of sorrow and unrest.

As night fell, the mansion seemed to come alive with a haunting energy. The shadows in the corners of the rooms grew darker and more pronounced, and the eerie sounds from the night before seemed to return. The friends huddled together, their sense of foreboding growing stronger.

The journal's entries and their ghostly encounter had deepened the mystery of the mansion. Priya, Aarav, Kavya, and Rohan knew they were only beginning to unravel the secrets of the estate. The spirits of the past were reaching out, and it was up to them to listen, understand, and uncover the truth.

As they settled in for the night, the weight of their discoveries pressed down on them. The mansion's oppressive silence seemed to amplify their fears, and the echoes of the past whispered through the cold, dark corridors. The ghosts of summer were not just figments of imagination—they were the echoes of a troubled history, waiting to be discovered and understood.

## Uncovering the Past

The library had become their sanctuary, but it also felt like a labyrinth of secrets waiting to be revealed. Priya, Aarav, Kavya, and Rohan were deeply engrossed in the journal, their faces illuminated by the flickering glow of a single desk lamp. The room was silent except for the occasional rustle of pages and the soft scratching of pens as they jotted down notes.

The journal was a treasure trove of information, detailing the lives of various occupants of the mansion over the centuries. Eleanor's entries provided a vivid picture of her life, her family, and the challenges they faced. But there were also references to other people—servants who had worked in the estate, visitors who had stayed briefly, and even some who had passed away under mysterious circumstances.

As Priya read through the faded entries, she noticed recurring themes of loss and sorrow. Each page seemed to whisper the stories of those who had lived and died within the mansion's walls. One entry, in particular, described the tragic death of a young girl named Anjali. Eleanor had written with a heavy heart about Anjali's untimely death and the impact it had on everyone in the household.

"This entry is heartbreaking," Priya said, her voice tinged with emotion. "It says that Anjali's death was a huge blow to the family. They were deeply affected by it."

Kavya leaned closer, her eyes scanning the lines. "There's mention of a fire that took Anjali's life, and it seems like it was shrouded in mystery. Some thought it was an accident, others believed it was something more sinister."

Aarav, who had been studying old census records, looked up. "I found a listing for Anjali's family. It seems they were quite prominent in the community. Her parents had a reputation for generosity, but they were devastated by the loss."

Rohan was flipping through a stack of old newspapers. "I came across an article about the fire. It describes how it destroyed a large part of the mansion and resulted in several fatalities. The article is vague about the cause, though, which makes me think there was more to it."

The group's curiosity was piqued. They realized that understanding Anjali's story was crucial to uncovering the mansion's secrets. They decided to visit the local town's archives, hoping to find more detailed records and personal accounts.

The Brooksville Historical Society was housed in a charming, albeit slightly dilapidated, brick building on the outskirts of town. Its exterior was adorned with ivy, and the front steps were worn from years of use. Inside, the air was thick with the scent of old paper and varnish, and the walls were lined with shelves filled with dusty volumes and faded photographs.

Mrs. Whitaker, the elderly archivist, welcomed them with a warm but weary smile. Her silver hair was neatly pinned up, and her glasses perched on the bridge of her nose as she led them to the archives.

"This is where we keep our historical records," she explained, gesturing to a room filled with filing cabinets, ledgers, and stacks of documents. "You might find what you're looking for in the old newspapers and personal records."

The teens set to work, combing through the archives. Priya and Kavya started with the newspaper clippings, hoping to find more information about the fire and its aftermath. Aarav and Rohan delved into census records and personal correspondence, searching for any references to Anjali and her family.

Hours passed as they sifted through the documents, their excitement growing with each new discovery. Priya found an old photograph of Anjali, her dark eyes and somber expression a haunting reminder of the tragedy. The photograph was accompanied by a small article about a memorial service held in her honor, highlighting the community's grief and the mystery surrounding her death.

"This photo must be from the time of the fire," Priya said, holding up the photograph. "It's clear that Anjali was cherished by those who knew her. The memorial service was a significant event."

Kavya, flipping through a dusty ledger, found an entry that mentioned Anjali's family. It detailed their financial struggles following the fire and the impact it had on their social standing. The ledger also hinted at rumors of negligence or foul play surrounding the incident.

"This ledger mentions financial difficulties and gossip about the fire," Kavya said. "It seems there were whispers of something more sinister, but no concrete evidence was ever found."

As they continued their research, an elderly man entered the archives. His presence was marked by an air of quiet dignity, and he carried a worn leather satchel. The man approached the group with a look of curiosity and concern.

"Excuse me," he said softly, "I couldn't help but overhear your conversation. Are you researching the old mansion?"

Priya looked up, surprised. "Yes, we are. Do you have any information about it?"

The man introduced himself as Mr. Thompson, a former groundskeeper of the mansion. His eyes held a deep well of memories as he spoke. "I worked at the mansion many years ago. There were always stories about the place—ghostly sightings, strange occurrences. The fire was a tragic event that left a mark on everyone who knew about it."

Mr. Thompson shared his recollections of the mansion's grandeur and the dark rumors that had surrounded it.

He spoke of how the estate had once been a thriving household, filled with laughter and warmth, but the fire had changed everything. He mentioned how the house had been abandoned for years after the tragedy, and how people believed the spirits of those who had died lingered in the shadows.

"Anjali's spirit," Mr. Thompson said quietly, "is said to wander the grounds, searching for peace. She was a beloved child who met an untimely end, and her story is deeply intertwined with the history of the mansion."

The group listened intently as Mr. Thompson handed them a few old photographs and personal notes he had kept over the years. These items provided additional context and helped piece together the mansion's troubled past.

As the sun began to set, casting long shadows through the dusty windows, the teens returned to the estate with their newfound knowledge. They gathered in the library, their minds abuzz with the revelations they had uncovered.

The journal, the newspaper articles, and Mr. Thompson's stories had painted a clearer picture of the mansion's history. The group realized that each ghostly encounter was part of a larger narrative, and their task was to unravel the past and help the spirits find resolution.

The weight of their discoveries pressed down on them as night fell. The mansion, with its creaking floors and whispering shadows, seemed to come alive with a haunting energy. The echoes of the past were stronger than ever, and the teens knew that their journey to uncover the truth was far from over.

## Haunting Intensifies

The once intriguing mysteries of the mansion had begun to escalate into a full-blown haunting. The spectral activity became more pronounced, and each ghost seemed increasingly determined to make contact with the teens. The mansion, with its creaking floors and shadowy corners, felt more like a living entity with its own secrets to reveal.

Aarav, often found in the study, had become accustomed to the chill that seemed to settle around him whenever he was alone there. However, his tolerance was tested one afternoon when the ghostly presence became more assertive. The once faint whispering now transformed into a full-fledged apparition.

While examining old military records and journals that he had collected from the study, Aarav noticed the air growing colder. The sound of distant gunfire and marching boots filled the room, though no one else was present. The ghostly figure of a soldier materialized by the window, his uniform tattered and stained, and his face marked by anguish and fatigue.

Aarav could see the soldier's spectral eyes were filled with a desperate longing. The soldier's ghost appeared to be trapped in a moment of historical conflict, unable to move on from his past. The soldier's eyes locked onto Aarav's, conveying an urgent plea for help.

"Please, find out what happened," the soldier's ghost implored in a voice that seemed to echo from a battlefield. "I need to know why I was left behind."

Aarav, though frightened, felt a surge of compassion. He began to search through the records more intently, looking for clues about the soldier's fate. Among the documents, he found a series of letters and a roster listing soldiers who had gone missing in action. There was a reference to a betrayal by someone within the ranks—a betrayal that had led to the soldier's capture and death.

Kavya's experience in the kitchen had been unsettling. The ghostly maid she encountered was not just an apparition but a woman with a deeply rooted sadness. The maid's spirit seemed tethered to the very fabric of the kitchen, lingering near the pantry where she had once spent countless hours.

As Kavya read through the diary and letters she had discovered, she pieced together the tragic story of the maid. The diary detailed the maid's life at the mansion, including her forbidden love affair with a young man of lower status. Their relationship had been scandalous, and when it was discovered, the maid faced severe repercussions.

One entry described the maid's final days with harrowing detail. She had been accused of theft—a crime she did not commit—as a way to cover up the true scandal of her affair. The letter she had found corroborated this, revealing that the maid had been unjustly punished and had died under mysterious circumstances.

Kavya felt the weight of the maid's betrayal and regret. The spirit's attachment to the kitchen and the pantry seemed to be a symbol of her life's final moments. Kavya decided to investigate further, seeking out records and talking to local historians who might have knowledge of the mansion's more obscure scandals.

Rohan's obsession with the attic had intensified. Every night, he felt an inexplicable pull towards the darkened space, and his visits became more frequent. The attic was cluttered with old furniture, forgotten relics, and dust-covered trunks.

During one of his nocturnal visits, Rohan encountered the shadowy figure he had seen previously. The figure was more defined now, its form exuding an air of melancholy and dread. The figure seemed to be guarding a large, ancient trunk that was situated in the corner of the attic.

Rohan approached the trunk cautiously. The figure's presence was almost palpable, casting an eerie light that seemed to shimmer with sorrow. As Rohan unlocked the trunk and began to sift through its contents, he found items that spoke of a forgotten past—a collection of letters, photographs, and a military uniform.

One photograph showed a group of soldiers and their families, but one face was scratched out. The items revealed connections to the soldier Aarav had encountered, including letters describing a betrayal and abandonment.

The trunk contained a letter from a soldier who had been wrongfully accused and subsequently abandoned. The soldier's fate had been sealed by a treacherous betrayal, which mirrored the story of the ghostly figure in the attic. Rohan realized that this figure was another victim of a similar injustice.

As night enveloped the mansion, Priya, Aarav, Kavya, and Rohan gathered in the library, their faces illuminated by the flickering light of candles. The weight of their experiences had brought them closer together, and they were united in their determination to solve the mysteries that plagued the mansion.

"We've all had intense encounters," Priya began, looking around at her friends. "The ghosts are more active now, and they seem desperate for us to uncover their stories."

Aarav shared his findings about the soldier's fate and the betrayal that led to his suffering. Kavya revealed the tragic tale of the maid's wrongful accusation and the cover-up of her affair. Rohan spoke of the trunk and its connection to both the soldier and the maid's stories.

"We need to address these issues," Aarav said, his voice firm. "The soldier's story of betrayal and the maid's injustice both need to be resolved. If we can uncover the full truth and expose the wrongs that were done, it might help these spirits find peace."

The group agreed that their next steps would involve digging deeper into the mansion's past, focusing on the unresolved issues and the people connected to the spirits they had encountered. They understood that resolving these issues would require more than just uncovering facts—it would involve confronting the ghosts' pain and helping them find closure.

As they prepared for another night of investigation, the mansion's eerie silence seemed to press in on them. The ghosts' stories were tangled in a web of betrayal and injustice, and unraveling this web would be crucial for bringing peace to the restless spirits and restoring harmony to the old family estate.

## Family Secrets

The revelations about Priya's great-great-grandmother, Sita Patel, had left an indelible mark on the group. The mansion's oppressive atmosphere seemed to mirror Priya's internal struggle as the once grand estate now felt more like a tomb of buried secrets.

Priya retreated to her room that evening, unable to shake off the weight of her discovery. The grand, old-fashioned decor of her room seemed to mock her turmoil with its grandeur and untouched elegance. The room felt like a relic from another era, much like the secrets she had just uncovered.

Sitting on the edge of her bed, Priya took out the letter again. Its faded ink and delicate paper were a stark contrast to the modern world she knew. She traced the words with her fingers, trying to connect with the emotions of her great-great-grandmother. Sita's plea for forgiveness felt like a ghostly whisper through time, begging Priya to understand the depth of the pain that had once plagued their family.

Her reflection in the mirror seemed foreign to her—a person caught between the past and present, struggling to reconcile the image of her family's legacy with the harsh reality of its hidden truths. Priya felt a deep sense of betrayal and confusion. How could her family have kept such a significant part of their history hidden? What did this mean for her identity and her place in the Patel lineage?

Determined to uncover more, Priya decided to dig deeper into the family's history. She approached Aarav,

Kavya, and Rohan with a new sense of purpose. "We need to find out everything about Sita Patel. Her story isn't just a tragic footnote; it's a crucial part of our family's legacy."

The group gathered in the library the next day, surrounded by old family records and letters. Aarav had brought along additional documents related to the soldier's story, hoping to find any connections to Priya's family. Kavya, driven by her empathy for the maid's plight, suggested looking into local archives for any records of scandal or injustice that might tie together with Sita's story.

As they pored over documents and discussed their findings, they began to piece together a more comprehensive picture of the mansion's past. Priya discovered that Sita's child—her great-grandparent—had been raised under a different name and had lived a life shrouded in secrecy. This child's existence had been meticulously hidden from public records, a deliberate act to erase any trace of the scandal.

With each new piece of information, the tensions among the group increased. The ghosts' stories had now intertwined with their own personal journeys, and the pressure of resolving these issues began to take its toll.

Aarav struggled with the idea that the soldier's betrayal might have involved a member of Priya's family, possibly even someone who had conspired to cover up Sita's scandal. The notion that his own family might have been complicit in such a dark history weighed heavily on him.

Kavya, who had been deeply moved by the maid's tragic fate, was particularly upset by the extent of the cover-up. She found it difficult to reconcile the injustices she had learned about with the present-day values she held dear.

Rohan, who had initially been the most practical of the group, was now finding it hard to focus. The connection between the trunk in the attic and the ghosts' stories seemed to be a metaphor for the layers of secrecy that had been buried over time. He felt overwhelmed by the weight of the mansion's dark history and struggled with the emotional toll it was taking on him.

The group decided to confront the present-day Patel family with their findings. Priya believed that in order to resolve the ghosts' unrest and move forward, they needed to face the truth head-on. She arranged a meeting with her parents and extended family, prepared to reveal the hidden scandal and its implications.

Sitting in the grand dining room of the mansion, Priya's parents and relatives listened in stunned silence as she recounted the details of Sita Patel's story. Priya's voice trembled, but she spoke with resolve. "We've uncovered a hidden part of our family's past—one that's been buried for over a century. Sita Patel's story is a part of our legacy, and it's time we confront it."

Her parents' reactions were a mixture of shock, guilt, and denial. Her mother struggled to process the information, while her father appeared uncomfortable, shifting in his seat. The family members exchanged uneasy glances, their discomfort evident.

Priya's father finally spoke up, his voice strained. "This is... unexpected. We were always taught to maintain our family's dignity. I didn't realize how deeply this history was buried."

Priya's mother added, "We never intended to hide the truth from you. It was more about protecting the family's reputation and keeping the past from overshadowing the present."

Priya, with tears in her eyes, replied, "But the past doesn't go away just because we ignore it. We need to face it, not just for ourselves, but for the spirits who are still trapped in this house."

After the family meeting, Priya felt a mix of relief and frustration. The confrontation had been necessary, but it hadn't been easy. The family's reaction showed that acknowledging the past was only the first step; healing and understanding would take time.

The group returned to the mansion, their resolve strengthened. They knew that their journey was far from over. The ghosts' stories were still incomplete, and the mansion's dark history needed to be fully addressed to bring peace to the restless spirits.

As they continued their investigation, Priya felt a newfound strength. The weight of her family's secret had been partially lifted, and she was determined to honor Sita Patel's legacy by uncovering the full truth and helping the spirits find their rest.

The mansion, with its haunting echoes and hidden stories, was more than just a backdrop for their journey; it was a testament to the complex interplay between the past and present, and the importance of confronting and reconciling with history.

## Confronting the Ghosts

As the summer drew to a close, the weight of the mansion's mysteries pressed heavily on Priya, Aarav, Kavya, and Rohan. They were now more determined than ever to help the restless spirits find peace. The haunting had intensified, and they knew they had to act quickly to resolve the ghosts' unfinished business.

The group gathered in the library, their sanctuary of old documents and haunted memories. The once inviting space now felt like a strategic command center for their efforts. Priya spread out the information they had gathered: journal entries, historical accounts, and personal experiences. They began to outline their plan.

"We need to address each spirit individually," Priya said, her voice filled with resolve. "We have to understand their stories completely and help them find the closure they need."

Aarav nodded. "We've learned a lot about the ghosts' pasts, but now we need to confront them directly. We should try recreating the key events from their lives to give them a chance to resolve their issues."

Kavya, who had been deeply affected by the maid's tragic story, suggested, "We should also perform rituals to help guide the spirits. Many cultures believe that rituals can aid in moving on from the earthly realm."

Rohan, always the practical thinker, added, "Let's document everything we do. We need to keep track of our progress and make sure we're addressing each ghost's specific needs."

The first spirit they decided to confront was Anjali, the young girl who had appeared to Priya. The group set up a makeshift séance in the parlor, using candles, incense, and a family heirloom that had belonged to Anjali. They hoped that these elements would create a connection to the spirit world.

Priya, holding the heirloom, called out to Anjali. "We're here to help you. Please show yourself if you're ready to talk."

The room grew cold, and the candles flickered. Anjali's ghost appeared, her form faint but clear. She looked sad but hopeful.

"Anjali, we know you're frightened and lost," Priya said gently. "Can you tell us what happened to you?"

Anjali's ghost began to relay her story in fragmented whispers. She spoke of a family feud that had led to her untimely death, a result of a tragic accident that had been dismissed as an unfortunate mishap. The spirit's family had never learned the truth, and Anjali had been left with a lingering sense of injustice.

To help Anjali, the group decided to recreate a pivotal moment from her life—an event that had caused her great sorrow. They arranged a small memorial in the garden, including elements that Anjali had cherished in life. Priya and the others spoke to her ghost, reassuring her that her story would be told and that her family would finally know the truth.

Next, they turned their attention to the soldier's ghost who had confronted Aarav. The soldier had been a young man who had fought in a forgotten war, only to return home and be shunned for his involvement. Aarav, feeling a personal connection to the soldier's sense of betrayal, took the lead in addressing his story.

The group set up a reenactment in the mansion's old dining hall, creating a scene that resembled the soldier's homecoming. They placed old military artifacts, uniforms, and letters in the room, hoping to evoke a sense of familiarity for the spirit.

As they called out to the soldier, his ghost appeared, appearing both solemn and relieved. Aarav spoke to him, sharing his own feelings of betrayal and injustice, hoping to empathize with the soldier's plight. The soldier's ghost revealed that he had been falsely accused of treason, and his name had been tarnished long after his death.

To help him, Aarav and the group worked to correct the historical record. They reached out to local historians and archivists, ensuring that the soldier's contributions were recognized and his name cleared. The soldier's ghost seemed to find solace in the acknowledgment of his sacrifices.

Kavya took on the task of addressing the maid's spirit, who had harbored a deep secret. The maid had been wronged by a powerful family member and had died with her grievances unaddressed. Kavya felt a strong connection to the maid's plight and was determined to right the wrongs she had suffered.

The group recreated the maid's living quarters, placing items that reflected her life and work. They performed a ritual of cleansing and forgiveness, hoping to offer the maid a chance to voice her grievances and find peace.

The maid's ghost appeared, her expression one of sadness but also relief. She revealed that her story involved an affair with a prominent family member, which had led to her being unfairly dismissed and left in poverty. The ritual allowed her to confront the injustices she had faced and seek forgiveness from those she felt had wronged her.

Meanwhile, Rohan continued his investigation into the attic. The mysterious figure he had sensed there turned out to be connected to the mansion's architectural changes. He discovered that the attic had once been a hidden room used for illicit activities and secret meetings. The presence that loomed there was linked to a tragic event—a betrayal that had resulted in the deaths of several individuals.

Rohan worked with the group to recreate the hidden room's original state. They discovered letters and artifacts that helped them piece together the events that had transpired. The ghost associated with the attic revealed its identity as a guardian of secrets who had been wronged by those who used the mansion for their own gain.

As they continued their efforts, the group worked to address each spirit's unresolved issues. They performed rituals, recreated historical scenes, and offered the spirits a chance to tell their stories. Each ghost began to show signs of relief and contentment as their stories were acknowledged and addressed.

The mansion, once a place of sorrow and unrest, started to feel lighter. The oppressive atmosphere lifted, and the ghosts appeared more at peace. The group had succeeded in helping the spirits find the closure they needed, and the mansion began to feel like a place of healing rather than one of haunting.

As the summer drew to a close, Priya, Aarav, Kavya, and Rohan felt a deep sense of accomplishment. They had faced their fears, confronted the past, and helped the spirits find peace. Their experiences had not only transformed the mansion but also deepened their understanding of themselves and each other.

The ghosts of summer had finally found their rest, and the mansion, with its dark history, had become a symbol of reconciliation and healing.

## Final Resting Place

As summer approached its end, the mansion, once a place of eerie unrest, now brimmed with anticipation and determination. The final spirit they needed to confront was the most formidable—a vengeful ancestor whose malevolence had cast a dark shadow over the estate for generations. The group, exhausted yet resolute, knew that confronting this spirit was critical to lifting the curse that had plagued the mansion.

The night before the final confrontation, Priya, Aarav, Kavya, and Rohan gathered in the library, the epicenter of their research and planning. The room, once a quiet space for studying, now felt like a war room—a place where their collective knowledge and experiences would culminate in their last attempt to free the mansion from its malevolent grip.

Priya, studying the journal entries and notes they had accumulated, addressed her friends. "Tomorrow will be the hardest part of our journey. This spirit is powerful and bound by centuries of anger. We need to be united and prepared."

Kavya, holding a ritual guide, added, "We've learned a lot about what might help this spirit find peace. We'll use everything we've gathered—rituals, historical reenactments, and personal connections. Our goal is to show this spirit that it's time to let go."

Aarav, who had taken a personal interest in the soldier's spirit, spoke up. "We need to remind the ancestor of their humanity. They've been consumed by their own anger and pain. If we can reach that part of them, maybe we can help them move on."

Rohan, who had been researching protective symbols and barriers, said, "I've reinforced the wards around the mansion. We're ready, but we need to stay focused and respectful. This spirit has been here a long time, and its power is immense."

As twilight fell, the mansion took on an almost palpable tension. The grand hall, where the final confrontation would take place, was prepared with the utmost care. The group arranged candles, symbols, and artifacts related to the spirit's past, hoping to create a bridge between their world and the spirit realm.

They set up a central altar with items significant to the ancestor's life: an ornate family crest, letters, and artifacts from the era in which the spirit lived. The group performed a preliminary ritual to create a protective circle around the room, ensuring their safety and maintaining focus.

With everything in place, the group stood in the grand hall, their emotions a mix of determination and apprehension. Priya took a deep breath and began the ritual, her voice steady despite the cold, charged air around them.

"We are here to offer you peace," Priya called out, her tone calm but commanding. "We know you've been wronged and that your pain has kept you bound to this place. It's time to find release."

The room grew colder, and shadows seemed to coalesce into a formidable form. The malevolent spirit of the ancestor appeared, its presence more intense and terrifying than anything they had faced before. The spirit's eyes burned with a fierce, unyielding anger.

"You dare to challenge me?" the spirit roared, its voice echoing like thunder. "I am the master of this place, and I will not be dismissed!"

Kavya stepped forward, her voice unwavering. "We understand your anger. You have been wronged, but continuing this path of vengeance will not bring you justice. It only perpetuates the suffering."

The spirit's gaze shifted to Kavya, its anger flickering with confusion. "You speak of justice and suffering, but these are concepts that were denied to me!"

Aarav, who had been deeply affected by the soldier's spirit, took a step closer. "We know that your pain is real, but holding onto it only traps you in a cycle of hatred. We've seen how much you've suffered, and we want to help you find the closure you've been denied."

To bridge the gap between the past and the present, the group decided to recreate a key event from the ancestor's life—a pivotal moment that had contributed to their anger. They transformed the grand hall into a scene reminiscent of the era, complete with period-appropriate décor and symbols.

As they set the scene, they spoke to the spirit, recounting the events that had led to its anger. They offered a perspective of understanding and forgiveness, trying to reach the part of the spirit that still held onto its humanity.

With the scene set, Priya led the group in a comprehensive cleansing ritual. The ritual involved invoking elements that represented both the positive and negative aspects of the spirit's past. They used symbols of peace, forgiveness, and acknowledgment, hoping to resonate with the spirit's history.

The air grew heavy with energy as the ritual progressed. Priya and her friends chanted ancient words, lighting candles and placing offerings on the altar. The spirit's form wavered, its anger slowly giving way to an expression of sorrow and resignation.

As the ritual reached its climax, the spirit's intense form began to dissolve. The room's oppressive atmosphere lifted, replaced by a sense of tranquility. The ancestor's vengeful anger had been tempered by the group's compassion and understanding.

The spirit looked at Priya and her friends with a mixture of relief and sadness. "You have shown me what I could not see. My anger was my own prison. I am ready to leave this place."

With a final, soft sigh, the spirit dissipated, leaving behind a calm and peaceful atmosphere. The mansion, once heavy with the weight of its dark history, began to feel lighter and more welcoming.

As the sun rose on the final day of their summer, Priya, Aarav, Kavya, and Rohan reflected on their journey. The mansion, now a place of peace, stood as a testament to their courage and empathy.

The group gathered in the grand hall, their faces illuminated by the morning light. They shared a quiet moment of reflection, recognizing how much they had grown through their experiences.

"We did it," Priya said softly, her voice filled with gratitude. "We've helped the spirits find their rest and transformed this place into something beautiful."

Aarav, looking around at the now serene mansion, added, "We've not only helped them but also ourselves. This experience has changed us in ways we couldn't have imagined."

Kavya and Rohan nodded in agreement. Their bond had grown stronger through their shared trials, and they knew that the lessons they had learned would stay with them for a lifetime.

As they prepared to leave the mansion, Priya and her friends felt a profound sense of accomplishment. The ghosts of the past had finally found their resting place, and the mansion was no longer a symbol of sorrow but of reconciliation and healing.

The final chapter of their summer had been written, but the impact of their journey would endure. The mansion, now a place of peace, stood as a reminder of the importance of confronting the past, understanding others, and finding closure.

Priya, Aarav, Kavya, and Rohan left the estate with a sense of fulfillment and hope. They had faced their fears, helped others find peace, and discovered their own inner strength. Their summer had been one of transformation, and the legacy of their journey would live on in the mansion's newfound tranquility.

## New Beginning

The once foreboding estate now seemed like a different world. The oppressive aura that had haunted the grand halls had been replaced with a gentle tranquility. As the sun filtered through the freshly cleaned windows, it illuminated the intricate details of the mansion's architecture—details that had been hidden under layers of dust and cobwebs.

The garden, once overgrown and wild, was now a vibrant tapestry of colors. The teens spent their days tending to the flower beds, planting new roses, and trimming the hedges. They discovered that the estate had a rich history of horticulture, with rare and exotic plants that had been neglected over the years. Rehabilitating the garden became a cherished project, a symbol of the renewal that was happening both inside the house and within themselves.

In their free time, Priya and her friends found solace in exploring different parts of the mansion. Priya, in particular, spent long hours in the library, once a room of hidden secrets and ghostly whispers. With the spirits at peace, the library felt like a sanctuary of knowledge and tranquility. She sifted through the old books and letters, uncovering more about her ancestors' contributions and achievements. This newfound connection to her heritage gave her a profound sense of pride and belonging.

Aarav took to the mansion's grand ballroom, where he practiced playing the old, dusty piano that had once been a centerpiece of the estate's social gatherings. The music that filled the room was no longer eerie or melancholic but resonant with hope and renewal. He began composing a piece inspired by the summer's experiences, a tribute to the estate's journey from darkness to light.

Kavya found herself drawn to the mansion's various art pieces, including portraits of the past residents. She spent time sketching and painting the restored rooms and gardens, capturing their transformation and the stories they held. Her artwork became a visual chronicle of the summer's events and a testament to the estate's new beginning.

Rohan, always the pragmatic one, focused on organizing the estate's archives and documents. He compiled a comprehensive history of the mansion, documenting the work they had done to uncover the past and restore the present. His detailed records would serve as a reference for future generations, ensuring that the estate's history and their efforts would not be forgotten.

Before they left, the teens organized a ceremony to celebrate the estate's rebirth and honor the lives of those who had once lived there. They invited local residents, many of whom had shared their knowledge and stories throughout the summer. The ceremony was held in the mansion's newly restored grand hall, where the atmosphere was now one of celebration rather than sorrow.

The ceremony began with a procession through the gardens, where guests admired the rejuvenated landscape. The teens had arranged for a selection of traditional dishes and refreshments, including some of the recipes they had discovered from the estate's past. As people gathered, the air was filled with laughter, conversation, and a sense of community.

Priya took the stage to address the crowd. Her speech was heartfelt and reflective, acknowledging the journey they had undertaken and the lessons they had learned. "This summer has been one of profound change, not just for us, but for this estate and the memories it holds. We've worked hard to honor the past and bring peace to the spirits who once haunted these halls. I hope that the lessons we've learned about family, legacy, and the importance of remembering our history will continue to resonate here."

The ceremony included a symbolic act of placing a commemorative plaque in the grand hall, inscribed with the names of those who had contributed to the estate's restoration. The plaque was a tribute to the spirits who had found peace and a reminder of the summer's impact.

As the summer drew to a close, the teens felt a mixture of satisfaction and melancholy. The estate had become a second home, a place of discovery and growth. The friendships they had forged were now deep and meaningful, and the experiences they shared had shaped their perspectives in ways they hadn't anticipated.

On their final night at the estate, the group gathered in the restored garden for a farewell bonfire. They reminisced about their adventures, the challenges they had overcome, and the bonds they had built. The crackling fire and the starry sky above created a sense of closure and serenity.

Priya, looking around at her friends, said, "This place has become a part of us. It's hard to say goodbye, but I'm grateful for everything we've experienced together."

Aarav nodded, adding, "We came here to solve a mystery and ended up finding so much more. We've grown as individuals and as friends."

Kavya smiled, her eyes reflecting the firelight. "The estate has taught us that even the darkest places can be illuminated with hope and understanding. I'll carry that lesson with me forever."

Rohan, with a final glance at the mansion, said, "We've left our mark here, and the estate will continue to be a place of peace and reflection. It's time for us to move on, but this summer will always be a part of who we are."

As they drove away from the estate, Priya, Aarav, Kavya, and Rohan looked back one last time. The mansion, now a symbol of their journey and transformation, stood proudly against the setting sun. The road ahead was filled with possibilities, and they knew that the summer had prepared them for the challenges and adventures that awaited.

The experiences of the past few months had taught them about bravery, empathy, and the importance of honoring the past. The lessons they had learned and the friendships they had formed would guide them as they continued their lives, carrying with them the spirit of the estate and the knowledge that they had made a lasting impact.

As the car drove into the horizon, the estate faded from view, but the memories and the growth they had experienced would remain with them forever, shaping their futures in ways they had yet to fully understand.

* * * * *

# EMOTIONAL MAP

## Discovery

Nina Patel had always been a bit of a skeptic when it came to family lore and old stories. But today, as she was tasked with cleaning out her grandmother's attic, she found herself immersed in a world of dusty memories and long-forgotten treasures. The attic was a sprawling space, filled with layers of history covered in a thick layer of dust. It smelled of cedar and aged paper, with faint traces of mothballs lingering in the air.

She moved methodically, sorting through old trunks and boxes that seemed to hold an endless array of antiques. The space was dimly lit by a single, dirty window that let in narrow beams of sunlight, illuminating the floating motes of dust. As she pushed aside a particularly heavy box, she uncovered an old, ornate wooden chest. Its dark mahogany surface was intricately carved with swirling patterns and floral motifs, hinting at an artistry from a bygone era.

Nina carefully pried open the chest, its hinges creaking in protest. Inside, she found an assortment of items: crumpled letters tied with yellowing ribbons, faded photographs of people she didn't recognize, and delicate laces that felt like they might disintegrate if touched too roughly. Nestled among these was a rolled-up parchment, secured with a frayed blue ribbon. The parchment was slightly yellowed with age but still held a sense of importance.

With a mixture of curiosity and reverence, Nina untied the ribbon and unrolled the parchment. The map that emerged was unlike anything she had ever seen. It was a detailed and elaborate representation of her town, but it was overlaid with a complex web of colors that seemed to pulse subtly. The map was not static; its colors shifted and flowed as if alive, transitioning from deep blues and purples to vibrant reds and greens.

Each section of the map was marked with a different emotional state. The colors were not uniform but varied in intensity and hue, indicating fluctuations in the emotional atmosphere of those areas. For example, a deep blue covered a part of town, while a bright yellow illuminated another. The map seemed to indicate not only physical locations but also the emotional climate of those who lived there.

Nina's fascination grew as she traced her finger over the map. It was not just a static representation but an interactive one, responding to her touch. Her mind raced with questions—how could a map show emotions? What was its purpose?

Her thoughts were interrupted by the creak of the attic door. Nina turned to see a tall figure standing in the doorway, his presence casting a long shadow across the dusty floor. The man was dressed in a dark, old-fashioned coat and wore a wide-brimmed hat that obscured his face. The dim light made his features hard to discern, but his eyes, a striking shade of gray, seemed to pierce through the darkness.

"Be careful with that map," the man said, his voice low and filled with an eerie resonance. "It's more than just a guide. It reveals the emotional landscapes of those who live in these areas. It's a tool of great power, and with that power comes great responsibility."

Before Nina could react or question him, the man turned and walked away, his footsteps echoing softly until they faded. The door closed behind him, leaving Nina alone with her thoughts and the enigmatic map.

The warning lingered in her mind, mingling with her curiosity and excitement. Despite the unsettling encounter, Nina felt compelled to explore the map's potential. She decided to investigate the areas marked with various emotional states, hoping to understand how the map functioned and what it revealed about the world around her.

The first area she chose to visit was marked with a deep, melancholic blue. As she walked through this part of town, she noticed subtle changes in her surroundings. The vibrant colors of the shops and houses seemed muted, and the usual bustle of the streets was replaced by an almost palpable sense of sadness. The atmosphere felt heavier, as though it was permeated by the collective emotions of the people living there.

Nina's exploration led her to a small park, where she saw an elderly woman sitting alone on a bench. The woman's posture was hunched, and her gaze was fixed on the ground. The sadness in her eyes was evident, matching the blue hue on the map. Nina approached her cautiously, feeling a mix of empathy and trepidation.

"Hello," Nina said softly, trying to offer a friendly smile. "Is everything okay?"

The woman looked up, her eyes clouded with grief. She hesitated before speaking, her voice trembling. "My husband passed away a few months ago," she said, her voice barely above a whisper. "I'm still trying to find my way without him."

Nina listened with a heavy heart, offering words of comfort and understanding. She shared some of her own experiences, hoping to provide a small measure of solace. As they spoke, Nina noticed a subtle change in the atmosphere around her. The deep blue of the map seemed to lighten slightly, and the park's ambiance shifted from oppressive to more serene.

Nina left the park with a sense of accomplishment but also with a multitude of questions. The map seemed to respond to her actions, indicating that it was more than just a static artifact. It was a dynamic tool that revealed and possibly influenced the emotional states of the people it depicted.

Returning home, Nina felt a mixture of excitement and apprehension. The map held the promise of discovery and personal growth, but it also carried a weight of responsibility. She poured over the journal she had found with the map, filled with cryptic notes about emotional states and personal growth, trying to decipher its meaning and understand her role in this unfolding journey.

With the map in hand and a burgeoning sense of purpose, Nina prepared for what lay ahead. The path was uncertain, but she felt ready to explore the emotional landscapes revealed by the map and uncover the deeper truths about herself and the world around her.

## First Journey

Nina Patel woke up early the next morning, her anticipation for her first journey guided by the mysterious map palpable. She had spent the previous night poring over the map and journal, trying to understand their connection and significance. The deep blue hue marking the town of Greenfield indicated a pervasive sadness that Nina felt compelled to explore.

After a quick breakfast, she gathered her things: a weathered notebook for jotting down observations, a few snacks, a bottle of water, and a camera to document any interesting findings. She carefully folded the map and placed it in her backpack, feeling a mix of excitement and apprehension. This was the start of something unusual and profound, and Nina was ready to embrace the journey.

The drive to Greenfield was serene but quiet. As she left the city behind and entered the rural landscape, the change in scenery mirrored the emotional tone of the map. Rolling fields and small clusters of houses came into view, with the overcast sky casting a grayish pallor over everything. Nina noted the muted hues of the landscape seemed to match the deep blue of the map, adding to the eerie sense of foreboding.

Upon arriving in Greenfield, Nina felt a palpable shift in the atmosphere. The usually bustling streets of a small town were unusually calm. Storefronts that would typically be lively were now closed or had their blinds half-drawn. The few pedestrians she saw walked slowly, their expressions somber. It was as if the whole town was enveloped in a collective shroud of sadness.

Nina parked her car near the town square, a central location that seemed to be a hub for community activity. The square was lined with quaint shops and cafés, but today they seemed to exude an air of desolation. The café she had decided to visit, "The Morning Brew," was no exception. Its once-vibrant awning was faded, and the bell above the door jingled with a melancholy tone as she stepped inside.

The café's interior was a contrast to its exterior—a cozy space with warm wooden tables, mismatched chairs, and walls lined with local art. However, the usual cheerful ambiance was replaced by a heavy silence. The air was thick with a sense of lingering grief, and the muted lighting only added to the somber atmosphere.

Nina scanned the room, looking for anyone who might embody the emotional state indicated by the map. At the counter, she spotted Alex—his disheveled appearance and vacant gaze immediately drew her attention. He was a tall teenager, with tousled hair and an expression that seemed lost in his own world. His clothes were casual but slightly rumpled, adding to his overall sense of defeat.

Nina approached Alex's table cautiously, not wanting to intrude but feeling a deep urge to connect. "Hi," she began, her voice gentle and reassuring. "I'm Nina. I couldn't help but notice you seem a bit down. Is everything okay?"

Alex looked up, startled by the sudden intrusion into his solitude. His eyes, red-rimmed and weary, met Nina's with a mixture of surprise and caution. "I'm just... struggling," he admitted after a moment of silence. "My brother recently passed away, and I don't really know how to deal with it."

Nina's heart ached for him. "I'm so sorry for your loss," she said softly. "It's really hard to go through something like this alone. If you want to talk, I'm here to listen."

Alex hesitated but then seemed to find solace in Nina's genuine offer. He began to open up about his brother, sharing stories about their childhood, their close bond, and the void that had been left behind. As he spoke, Nina listened with empathy, occasionally nodding or offering gentle words of support. She spoke from her own experiences with loss, trying to offer some comfort and practical advice.

During their conversation, Nina noticed subtle changes in Alex's demeanor. The heaviness that had weighed on him seemed to lift slightly, and a small glimmer of hope appeared in his eyes. Nina encouraged him to consider honoring his brother's memory through activities like creating a scrapbook or writing letters. She suggested seeking support from friends, family, or a counselor, emphasizing that it was okay to ask for help.

As Nina prepared to leave, she observed the café's ambiance. The once oppressive sadness seemed to have lightened, and the café felt a little warmer and more welcoming. The colors of the room appeared to shift subtly, echoing the lighter mood.

Nina took a moment to check the map before heading out. She was astonished to see that the deep blue hue over Greenfield had faded to a softer, more hopeful tone. The change in the map's colors confirmed her sense that her actions had made a difference.

Driving back home, Nina reflected on her experience. The map wasn't just a tool for observing emotional states; it was a catalyst for change. Her interactions with Alex had not only helped him begin to heal but had also transformed the emotional landscape of the town.

Nina's sense of purpose was stronger than ever. She was eager to see where the map would lead her next, knowing that each journey had the potential to affect the lives of those she encountered and to deepen her understanding of the human experience. The road ahead was uncertain, but she felt prepared to embrace whatever challenges and discoveries lay in store.

## Unexpected Connections

Nina Patel felt a renewed sense of excitement as she prepared for her next journey. The map had led her to a vibrant yellow area, suggesting a state of creativity and optimism that had been overshadowed by underlying challenges. The brightness of the yellow hue intrigued her, hinting at potential growth and renewal.

The town she arrived in was called Crestview, known for its lively arts scene and colorful murals. As Nina drove through the streets, she was struck by the vividness of the surroundings. The town was adorned with creative expressions—from painted storefronts to artistic sculptures scattered throughout the public spaces. Despite the vibrant environment, Nina couldn't shake the feeling that something was amiss.

Her destination was an old warehouse that had been converted into an art studio. The building stood out with its bright yellow facade and large windows, though the energy seemed subdued from the outside. Nina entered the studio and was greeted by the sight of various unfinished paintings and sculptures. The studio's atmosphere was a mix of creative chaos and quiet introspection.

In one corner of the studio, Nina spotted Lila—a young woman in her mid-twenties, surrounded by half-completed canvases and scattered art supplies. Lila's appearance was a stark contrast to the bright surroundings; her expression was one of frustration and sadness. She was hunched over a canvas, her paintbrush moving hesitantly as if the creative spark she once had was now buried under a weight of self-doubt.

Nina approached cautiously, sensing Lila's internal struggle. "Hi," she said gently, "I'm Nina. I couldn't help but notice your beautiful art. It looks like you're working on something special."

Lila glanced up, her eyes filled with a mix of surprise and weariness. "Oh, hi," she replied, her voice lacking enthusiasm. "I'm Lila. I used to be really passionate about painting, but lately, I just can't seem to find my inspiration. It's like I've hit a wall, and I'm scared that I'm losing my touch."

Nina could see the sadness in Lila's eyes and the way her shoulders slumped as she spoke. "I understand," Nina said empathetically. "Sometimes, when we face self-doubt, it can be really hard to move forward. What do you usually do when you're feeling stuck?"

Lila sighed deeply, setting down her paintbrush. "I used to paint every day, but now I just... hesitate. I'm afraid that whatever I create won't be good enough, and that fear just paralyzes me."

Nina thought for a moment before responding. "You know, I've been on this journey where I help people based on the emotions marked on this map I found. It's been fascinating to see how interconnected our feelings can be. It sounds like you're dealing with fear and self-doubt, which is affecting your creativity."

Lila looked intrigued but skeptical. "That's an interesting way to look at it. But how do you deal with something like this?"

Nina offered a comforting smile. "Sometimes, it helps to talk through your fears and remember why you started in the first place. It's also important to give yourself permission to create without judgment. Art is a way of expressing yourself, not just a product to be critiqued."

Encouraged by Nina's words, Lila opened up about her journey as an artist—her early successes, the pressures she faced, and the internal conflicts that had led to her current state of hesitation. Nina listened attentively, offering insights and encouragement. She suggested that Lila try creating art in a more experimental way, without worrying about the end result. The idea was to reconnect with the joy of creation itself.

Over the following days, Nina and Lila spent time together in the studio. Nina would occasionally join Lila in painting, and they talked about their experiences and aspirations. Nina's presence brought a renewed energy to the studio. Lila began to approach her work with a fresh perspective, gradually letting go of her fears and embracing the process of creation.

One afternoon, as Nina was preparing to leave, she noticed a significant change in Lila's demeanor. The artist had completed several new pieces, each more vibrant and expressive than the last. Lila's confidence had visibly returned, and her smile was genuine and full of pride.

"I can't thank you enough," Lila said sincerely. "You've helped me remember why I fell in love with painting in the first place. I'm excited to see where this new direction takes me."

Nina felt a profound sense of fulfillment as she observed the transformation in Lila. The yellow hue on the map seemed to shimmer with renewed brightness, reflecting Lila's regained passion and confidence. Nina realized that her efforts had not only helped Lila reconnect with her creativity but had also illuminated the interconnected nature of human emotions.

As Nina left Crestview, she reflected on her growing understanding of how emotions could influence and be influenced by those around us. Each person she encountered seemed to be a piece of a larger puzzle, and her actions were creating ripple effects that extended far beyond individual encounters.

With the map as her guide, Nina was eager to see where her journey would take her next. Each town, each person, and each emotional state had the potential to reveal deeper insights into the human experience, and she was ready to embrace whatever came next with an open heart.

## Emotional Turmoil

Nina Patel's map guided her to a small town marked in a deep, intense red, a color that signaled high emotional turmoil. The vivid red hue seemed to pulse with the weight of unresolved anger and frustration, hinting at a place where deep-seated issues were brewing.

As she arrived in the town of Riverton, Nina was struck by its quiet, almost subdued atmosphere. The red zone's emotional intensity seemed to contrast sharply with the peaceful suburban streets and neat homes. There was a sense of unease that permeated the air, a silent tension that was palpable even before she met the person at the heart of it.

Nina's search led her to Riverton High School, where she found Jason—a seventeen-year-old student whose anger and frustration seemed to radiate from him. Jason's demeanor was marked by a defiant attitude, and he was often seen arguing with teachers or distancing himself from his peers. Nina learned that Jason's struggles were deeply rooted in his relationship with his family, who had high expectations for his academic and extracurricular achievements.

One afternoon, as Nina sat in a local café reflecting on her observations, she saw Jason storm in, clearly agitated. He ordered a coffee with a huff and took a seat by himself, slamming his backpack onto the table. Nina took a deep breath and decided to approach him, sensing that he might be the key to understanding the emotional turmoil of the town.

"Hey, Jason," Nina said, trying to sound casual and friendly. "Mind if I join you?"

Jason looked up, his face a mixture of surprise and irritation. "Sure, whatever," he replied, his tone flat.

Nina sat down and observed him carefully. "I couldn't help but notice that you seem really stressed. If you want to talk about it, I'm here to listen."

Jason's expression hardened for a moment, but then he sighed heavily. "I don't know what's the point. My family just doesn't get it. They expect me to be perfect—straight A's, sports, all of it. I feel like I'm constantly being pushed to be something I'm not. It's exhausting."

Nina nodded empathetically. "That sounds incredibly tough. It's hard when people have expectations for us that feel impossible to meet. What do you really want to do, Jason? What makes you happy?"

Jason's eyes widened slightly, and he looked down at his coffee. "I used to love playing guitar. But lately, I haven't had the time or energy for it. I'm too busy trying to live up to everyone else's standards."

Nina listened intently, understanding the weight of Jason's struggles. "It sounds like you're caught in a cycle of trying to meet others' expectations while losing sight of your own passions and desires. Sometimes, talking about these feelings with someone can help, and finding a balance between what others want and what you need for yourself is important."

Jason was silent for a moment, contemplating Nina's words. He took a sip of his coffee and seemed to relax slightly. "I've been so focused on making everyone else happy that I forgot about myself. Maybe I do need to make some changes."

Nina suggested that Jason start by setting aside time each day to reconnect with his guitar, even if it was just for a short while. She also encouraged him to communicate his feelings with his family, explaining that they might not fully understand his perspective but that expressing his needs could help in bridging the gap between their expectations and his own aspirations.

Over the next few days, Nina observed a gradual change in Jason. He began to take small steps toward reclaiming his passion for music. He practiced playing the guitar in the evenings, and Nina could see a renewed spark in his eyes when he spoke about it. His interactions with his family also started to shift. He tried to express his feelings more openly, and while it wasn't always smooth, there was a noticeable effort to bridge the emotional gap that had existed for so long.

One evening, Nina watched from a distance as Jason performed at a local open mic night—a small, yet significant step in reconnecting with his love for music. The performance was heartfelt, and Jason's family, who had come to support him, watched with a mixture of pride and understanding.

As Nina left Riverton, she felt a profound sense of accomplishment. The emotional red zone on the map had begun to shift, reflecting Jason's progress in dealing with his anger and frustration. Nina realized that addressing deep-seated emotions wasn't easy and that it required patience and understanding.

The journey had taught her that emotions were complex and multifaceted, and helping people navigate their inner turmoil was a delicate process. Each person's struggle was unique, and the path to resolution often involved confronting uncomfortable truths and making difficult changes.

With her next destination already marked on the map, Nina was ready to face new challenges and continue her journey of emotional discovery. She understood that each town and each person held its own story, and she was prepared to delve deeper into the intricacies of human emotion as she moved forward on her path.

## Challenge of Empathy

Nina Patel's emotional map led her to the tranquil but seemingly troubled town of Everbrook, marked in a deep, distressing purple. The color indicated pervasive anxiety, and as Nina drove through the quiet streets, she could sense the undercurrent of unease that seemed to pervade the town. The houses were well-kept, and the gardens neatly trimmed, but there was an intangible sense of worry in the air.

Nina's search for the source of this anxiety brought her to a local café, a cozy spot with warm lighting and a comforting atmosphere. It was here that she encountered Sara—a young woman whose bright demeanor seemed to mask a deep-seated struggle. Sara was a talented artist known for her creativity, but lately, her life had been overshadowed by debilitating anxiety about the future.

Sara sat at a corner table, her face illuminated by the soft glow of a reading lamp. The table was cluttered with notebooks filled with sketches, lists, and scribbled thoughts, all of which seemed to weigh heavily on her. Sara's fingers drummed anxiously on her coffee cup, and her gaze was distant, lost in a whirlwind of worries.

Nina approached cautiously, her heart heavy with empathy for the woman whose distress she could feel even before speaking with her. "Hi, Sara," Nina began gently, taking a seat across from her. "I hope you don't mind if I join you. I've noticed you seem a bit overwhelmed. I'd love to listen if you'd like to talk."

Sara looked up, her eyes reflecting a mix of surprise and relief. "Oh, um, sure. I could use someone to talk to," she said, her voice tinged with exhaustion.

Nina offered a reassuring smile. "I'm here to listen. It sounds like you're dealing with a lot right now. What's been on your mind?"

Sara sighed deeply, her shoulders slumping as she finally allowed herself to express the weight she had been carrying. "I feel like I'm stuck in this endless cycle of worrying about the future. I've always been told that I need to have everything planned out perfectly—college, career, life goals. But no matter what I do, I never feel like I'm doing enough. It's like there's this constant pressure to be perfect, and it's paralyzing."

Nina nodded, her own sense of anxiety echoing Sara's. She recognized the familiar feeling of being overwhelmed by expectations, both self-imposed and external. "It sounds incredibly tough. I've felt similar pressures about my future, too. It's easy to get caught up in trying to meet everyone's expectations and lose sight of what really matters to you."

Sara's eyes filled with tears, and she looked down at her cluttered table. "I've been so consumed by fear of failing that I haven't been able to enjoy anything. I keep pushing myself to meet others' expectations, but it feels like I'm losing a part of myself in the process."

Nina's heart ached for Sara. She knew that addressing such deep-rooted anxiety required more than just talking—it required actionable steps to help Sara regain control over her life and her emotions. "Let's start by taking small steps. Sometimes breaking down big goals into manageable tasks can make them seem less daunting. What's one thing you've always wanted to do but haven't because of this fear?"

Sara thought for a moment, her gaze drifting to the sketches scattered across her table. "I've always wanted to pursue my art more seriously. I love painting, but I've been too afraid to dedicate time to it because I'm worried it won't lead to anything concrete."

Nina encouraged Sara to start small. "Why not set aside just a little bit of time each week to focus on your art? It doesn't have to be perfect or lead to something big right away. Just allowing yourself to explore your creativity can be a way to reconnect with what makes you happy."

Nina also suggested that Sara consider joining a local support group or finding a therapist to talk through her fears and develop coping strategies. They worked on building a support system, emphasizing the importance of sharing her struggles with trusted friends or family members who could offer encouragement and perspective.

Over the next few weeks, Nina saw Sara begin to implement these changes. Sara started dedicating a small corner of her apartment to her art, creating a space where she could escape the pressures of daily life and focus on what she loved. She began to take time for herself and even joined a local art class where she met others who shared her passion.

Nina observed Sara's growing confidence and sense of peace. The deep purple on the map, once a stark symbol of anxiety, began to shift towards lighter shades, reflecting Sara's progress. Sara's willingness to confront her fears and take steps towards her own happiness made a tangible difference.

One afternoon, Sara invited Nina to an art exhibit she had organized, showcasing her recent works. The event was a testament to Sara's growth and resilience. As she spoke about her journey and the art she had created, there was a newfound warmth and optimism in her voice.

Nina felt a profound sense of accomplishment. Helping Sara navigate her anxiety and reconnect with her passions had not only impacted Sara's life but had also deepened Nina's own understanding of empathy and personal growth. The experience had reminded Nina of the importance of facing one's fears and finding balance amidst the pressures of life.

As Nina prepared to leave Everbrook, she reflected on the emotional journey she had shared with Sara. The challenge of empathy had been both humbling and enlightening, teaching Nina valuable lessons about connection and support. With her next destination on the map awaiting, Nina was ready to continue her journey of emotional discovery, armed with newfound insights and a deeper appreciation for the complexities of human emotions.

## Emotional Map's Secrets

Nina Patel's journey took an unexpected turn when she revisited her grandmother's attic, driven by a growing curiosity about the map's origins and its connection to her family. The attic, once a place of dusty relics and forgotten memories, now felt like a treasure trove of clues about her family's hidden legacy.

With a sense of purpose, Nina carefully examined the old journal she had found alongside the map. The journal, weathered and yellowed with age, was filled with handwritten notes, sketches, and cryptic messages that seemed to provide a deeper understanding of the map's purpose. The entries were penned in a graceful script, and as Nina read through them, she discovered that the map was much more than a mere guide—it was a tool for emotional healing and personal growth.

The journal revealed that the map had been created by her great-grandmother, Mira Patel, who was renowned for her work in emotional and psychological healing. Mira had developed the map as a way to help people navigate their emotional landscapes, a concept that was revolutionary for its time. The map was said to reveal the emotional states of different regions and individuals, guiding those who used it towards greater empathy and understanding.

One particular entry caught Nina's eye:

*"The Emotional Map is not just a guide but a legacy. It has been passed down through generations, each caretaker adding their own insights and experiences. It is meant to bridge the gap between our emotions and our actions, allowing us to help others while also finding our own path to healing. Remember, the map's power lies in its ability to connect us with our deepest feelings and those of others."*

Nina's heart raced as she realized the gravity of her discovery. The map was not just a relic—it was a beacon of hope and healing that had been carefully preserved through her family's history. The journal also contained personal anecdotes from Mira's life, detailing how she had used the map to assist individuals in overcoming emotional struggles and finding balance in their lives.

Determined to honor her great-grandmother's legacy, Nina decided to delve deeper into the map's history and its impact on her family. She began to explore more of the journal's entries, which described various cases where the map had been used to help people navigate complex emotional challenges. Each story was a testament to the map's ability to bring about profound change, both for those it helped and for the family members who guided them.

One entry in particular stood out:

*"During the Great Depression, the map was instrumental in helping a community struggling with despair and hopelessness. By guiding individuals to confront their fears and connect with one another, the map brought light into the darkest of times. This is the true power of our legacy—transforming despair into hope and confusion into clarity."*

Nina was moved by the realization that the map had been a source of comfort and guidance during some of the most challenging times in history. She felt a renewed sense of responsibility and commitment to continue her journey, not just for herself but to honor the legacy of her ancestors.

With this newfound understanding, Nina set out to use the map's power more consciously. She approached her next destination with a greater sense of purpose, knowing that each journey was a chance to make a meaningful impact. The map's vibrant colors, which once seemed like mere indicators of emotions, now held a deeper significance. They represented the collective emotions of those she had met and the changes she had witnessed.

As Nina traveled to her next location, she carried with her the weight of her family's legacy and the hope of continuing the work that had begun so many years ago.

The emotional map was no longer just a guide; it was a bridge between the past and the present, connecting her with her great-grandmother's spirit and the timeless quest for emotional understanding and growth.

The journey ahead promised new challenges and revelations, but with each step, Nina felt more prepared to embrace the map's secrets and carry forward the legacy of emotional healing and empathy that had been passed down through generations.

## Facing the Darkest Emotions

Nina Patel's journey through the emotional map had been transformative, but nothing could have prepared her for the foreboding darkness of her next destination. The map had led her to an isolated, desolate area marked by deep shades of gray and black, representing a profound state of depression and despair. The atmosphere was heavy, and a sense of foreboding seemed to hang in the air.

As Nina approached the desolate area, she was struck by the oppressive silence that enveloped the landscape. The surroundings were stark and barren, with crumbling buildings and abandoned spaces that seemed to echo the emotional void that pervaded the region. Her heart pounded with apprehension, sensing that this would be her most challenging encounter yet.

At the center of this bleak landscape, Nina found Ethan, a young man who appeared to be living in near-complete isolation. His eyes were dull, and his posture slumped as if the weight of the world was pressing down on him. Ethan's presence was a stark contrast to the vibrant personalities

Nina had previously encountered; his struggle with severe depression was palpable.

Nina approached Ethan with a mix of empathy and trepidation. She introduced herself, but her words seemed to hang in the air, swallowed by the pervasive sense of hopelessness. Ethan looked at her with a mixture of curiosity and suspicion, his eyes revealing the depth of his inner turmoil.

"I don't know what you can do here," Ethan said quietly, his voice tinged with resignation. "I've been trying to fight this for so long, and nothing seems to make a difference."

Nina's heart ached for Ethan, and she felt the enormity of his despair weigh on her. The emotional intensity of the area seemed to seep into her own being, amplifying her fears and doubts. She found herself grappling with her own emotions—her earlier experiences had been challenging, but this was different. The darkness was almost palpable, and Nina felt a deep sense of inadequacy.

Determined to help Ethan, Nina began by listening. She sat with him in the empty, desolate space, allowing him to speak freely about his struggles. As Ethan shared his feelings of hopelessness and isolation, Nina realized that her role was not to offer quick fixes or superficial solutions but to provide genuine support and understanding.

Throughout their conversations, Nina discovered that Ethan's depression was rooted in a series of life events and personal losses that had compounded over time. His sense of isolation was not just physical but emotional, and he struggled to find meaning and purpose in his life.

Nina began to introduce small, practical steps to help Ethan. She encouraged him to reconnect with old hobbies and interests, which he had abandoned. She also suggested that he seek professional help, sharing resources and local support services that could provide him with the assistance he needed. Nina knew that while she could offer guidance and support, overcoming such profound emotional challenges required a multifaceted approach.

As she worked with Ethan, Nina also confronted her own fears and limitations. The darkness of the area seemed to reflect her internal struggles, and she had to face her own feelings of helplessness and vulnerability. Nina realized that empathy and support were not always straightforward; they required patience, understanding, and sometimes the courage to confront uncomfortable truths.

One evening, as the sun set and the sky turned a muted gray, Ethan tentatively agreed to start reaching out for help. He began to explore local support groups and therapy options, encouraged by Nina's unwavering support. It was a small but significant step toward healing, and Nina felt a glimmer of hope that things could improve.

The emotional atmosphere of the area began to shift slightly as Ethan's first steps toward recovery took shape. Nina noticed that the intense gray tones on the map started to lighten, reflecting the gradual change in Ethan's emotional state. The shift was subtle but meaningful, and it gave Nina a renewed sense of purpose.

As her time in the desolate area came to an end, Nina felt a mixture of relief and exhaustion. The journey had been one of her toughest yet, testing her resilience and empathy in profound ways. She left Ethan with a sense of cautious optimism, knowing that the path to healing was long and arduous but also possible.

Nina continued her journey with a deeper understanding of the complexity of human emotions. The map had revealed the darkest corners of despair, but it had also shown her the power of compassion and the importance of confronting and supporting those who were struggling. She carried with her the lessons learned from Ethan's story and prepared for the next chapter in her journey, ready to face whatever challenges lay ahead.

## Final Revelation

Nina Patel's journey had led her through a spectrum of emotions, from the deep blues of sadness to the fiery reds of anger, the vibrant yellows of creativity, and the somber grays of despair. As she followed the map one last time, it guided her to a central location where all these emotional hues converged. The area was a kaleidoscope of colors, a swirling tapestry that seemed to embody the complexity and depth of the human experience.

Arriving at this multifaceted place, Nina was struck by its profound beauty and overwhelming complexity. It was neither distinctly joyful nor sorrowful but a rich, dynamic blend of every emotion she had encountered throughout her journey. The landscape was a mosaic of vibrant and muted shades, reflecting the intricate interplay of human feelings.

In this central location, Nina found a gathering of individuals—people she had met on her previous journeys. Each person was surrounded by an aura that reflected their emotional states and the progress they had made. Alex, Lila, Jason, Sara, and Ethan were all there, along with others from the different emotional zones Nina had visited. The atmosphere was both familiar and new, a testament to the interconnectedness of their stories and emotions.

The reunion was poignant. As Nina approached her companions, she could see the changes they had undergone. Alex's grief was now tempered by acceptance and hope. Lila's creativity had blossomed, her vibrant energy illuminating the space. Jason had found ways to channel his anger into constructive communication with his family. Sara had developed a sense of calm and purpose, and Ethan, although still on his journey, showed signs of renewed hope and connection.

Together, the group began to explore this central space, each person contributing their own experiences and insights. They shared stories of their journeys, reflecting on how their emotions had shifted and evolved. As they spoke, Nina realized that the emotional map had not just guided her to individual people but had led her to a deeper understanding of the human condition.

The group decided to collaborate on a collective project, aiming to address their shared emotional wounds and build a supportive community. They created a large, collaborative mural that incorporated elements from each person's journey—symbols of healing, growth, and connection. As they worked together, they found solace in their shared experiences and the mutual understanding they had developed.

Nina and her companions also organized a series of workshops and discussions to facilitate open dialogue about their emotions. They invited others from the central location to join, encouraging a broader community to engage in collective healing. The workshops covered topics such as coping strategies, emotional resilience, and the importance of empathy. They created safe spaces for people to express their feelings and support one another.

The mural and the workshops became a focal point for the community, drawing people from all walks of life. The central location transformed into a vibrant hub of emotional healing and personal growth, a testament to the power of coming together to address and embrace the full spectrum of human emotions.

As Nina observed the positive changes taking place, she felt a profound sense of fulfillment. Her journey had brought her to this moment of collective revelation and healing. She realized that the emotional map had not only guided her through different emotional states but had also led her to a deeper understanding of the interconnectedness of human experiences.

The final revelation was not just about the resolution of individual stories but about the collective power of empathy and connection. The central location represented the heart of the human experience, where emotions blended and overlapped, creating a complex but beautiful tapestry of life.

As Nina prepared to leave the central location, she carried with her the lessons learned from her journey—the importance of acknowledging and embracing all emotions, the value of empathy, and the power of collective healing. She felt a renewed sense of purpose and hope, ready to continue her journey with a deeper understanding of the human experience.

The emotional map had led her through a transformative adventure, and as she looked back at the vibrant, interconnected landscape, Nina knew that her journey had only just begun.

## New Beginning

As Nina stands in the heart of the central emotional realm, she watches in awe as the map transforms before her eyes. The vivid, chaotic colors that once represented individual emotional states begin to harmonize into a more cohesive pattern. The once tumultuous landscape now glows with a gentle, calming light, reflecting areas of potential growth and healing.

The map's transformation signifies a profound shift not only in the way emotions are represented but also in Nina's understanding of her own journey. Each area is now marked with symbols of hope, potential, and interconnectedness, rather than the isolated emotional struggles she once saw.

With the map now indicating paths to emotional renewal rather than crises, Nina feels a renewed sense of purpose. She embarks on her journey back home, reflecting on the wisdom she has gained. The road ahead seems less daunting; she now carries with her a deeper understanding of human emotions and her own role in fostering positive change.

Upon arriving home, Nina is greeted with warmth by her family and friends. They notice a change in her demeanor—she radiates a calm confidence and a deeper empathy. Nina shares some of her experiences, though she keeps the details of the map's transformation close to her heart. She is eager to apply what she has learned to her own community.

Nina begins to implement her newfound knowledge in practical ways:

1. Emotional Wellness Workshops: Nina starts by organizing workshops focused on emotional wellness. These workshops are designed to help community members understand their own emotions, develop coping strategies, and build resilience. She invites local experts to speak about mental health, self-care, and the importance of emotional intelligence.

2. Community Support Groups: Recognizing the value of peer support, Nina establishes support groups where individuals can share their experiences and offer each other encouragement. These groups create a safe space for people to discuss their challenges and celebrate their progress.

3. Youth Programs: Understanding the importance of early education, Nina collaborates with schools to introduce programs that teach emotional literacy

and empathy to students. These programs include activities that promote self-awareness, emotional regulation, and effective communication.

4. Outreach and Advocacy: Nina becomes an advocate for mental health awareness in her community. She partners with local organizations to raise awareness about emotional health issues and to promote resources available for those in need.

Nina's efforts begin to make a visible impact. Community members show increased openness and willingness to discuss their feelings. The workshops and support groups foster a stronger sense of community, and the youth programs help build a foundation of emotional intelligence in the next generation.

As Nina watches the positive changes unfold, she realizes that her journey has not only transformed her own life but has also sparked a broader movement toward emotional well-being in her community. She witnesses firsthand how small acts of empathy and understanding can create ripple effects that benefit many.

On a personal level, Nina finds a deep sense of fulfillment and purpose. Her interactions with others are enriched by her experiences, and she approaches her relationships with greater insight and compassion. The emotional challenges she once faced seem more manageable now that she has the tools and understanding to navigate them.

With her community thriving and her personal growth solidified, Nina looks to the future with hope and excitement. The map, now a symbol of her journey and the positive change she has fostered, serves as a reminder of the potential within every person and every community to grow and heal.

Nina feels a profound connection to the broader human experience and is inspired to continue her journey of learning and growth. She knows that the path to emotional understanding and healing is ongoing, and she is ready to embrace the future with a renewed sense of purpose and possibility.

The chapter closes with Nina standing at the edge of her community, looking out at the horizon with a hopeful smile. She is prepared to take the lessons she has learned and the changes she has made and continue her mission to foster emotional well-being wherever she goes.

* * * *

# STORIES LEFT UNTOLD

## Unexpected Offer

Seventeen-year-old Emma had never believed in ghosts. But as she sat in the dimly lit attic of her family's new home, the chill running down her spine suggested otherwise. The attic was filled with forgotten relics—old trunks, moth-eaten clothes, and dusty books that hadn't seen the light of day in decades. Among the clutter, something caught her eye: an antique typewriter, its once-shiny surface now dulled by a thick layer of dust.

Curiosity piqued, Emma approached the typewriter, brushing off the dust to reveal ornate brass keys. She hesitated for a moment, then placed her fingers on the keyboard, pressing a key lightly. The machine clattered loudly in the silent attic, sending a shiver through her. But before she could react, the typewriter began to move on its own. Keys clicked furiously, typing out words that formed sentences—sentences that made no sense at first but quickly began to cohere into a coherent message.

Emma's heart raced as she watched the typewriter type out, "Hello, Emma. I've been waiting for you."

She stumbled back, nearly tripping over a stack of old books. The typewriter fell silent, but the words it had produced stared back at her from the yellowed paper. Her mind raced with questions, but before she could think too deeply, the room grew colder, and a faint, ghostly figure materialized before her.

The figure was an elderly man, dressed in an old-fashioned suit, his face lined with age but his eyes sharp and intelligent. He tipped his hat to her, a gesture that seemed oddly formal given the circumstances.

"Good evening, Emma," the ghostly figure said, his voice as smooth as silk. "I am Mr. Whitmore, and I believe we have some work to do."

Emma's eyes widened in disbelief, her voice caught in her throat. She had always considered herself a rational person, but here she was, standing in her attic, talking to a ghost.

"I... I don't understand," Emma stammered. "What is this? Who are you?"

Mr. Whitmore smiled kindly. "I am a ghostwriter, quite literally. My job is to write the final stories for those who have passed but have left something unsaid, something unfinished. Unfortunately, I've come to a point where I need assistance. And that's where you come in."

Emma's mind swirled with a hundred questions, but one stood out. "Why me? Why now?"

"You have a talent for words," Mr. Whitmore replied. "A gift that many of the departed need. You've also moved into this house, where the typewriter resides. Fate, it seems, has brought you here."

Emma was skeptical, but something about the situation—about Mr. Whitmore—intrigued her. She had always been drawn to stories, to uncovering hidden truths, and the idea of helping souls find peace resonated with her, even if it did sound absurd.

"What would I have to do?" she asked cautiously.

"Simple," Mr. Whitmore said, his ghostly form flickering slightly. "You would help me listen to the stories of the departed, those with unfinished business, and then write them down. By doing so, you help them move on, and in return, you'll learn more about the world beyond, about life, death, and everything in between."

Emma's skepticism lingered, but the offer was too strange and compelling to ignore. She couldn't shake the feeling that this was something she was meant to do. After a moment of silence, she nodded. "Okay. I'll do it."

Mr. Whitmore's smile widened. "Very good, my dear. We'll begin tomorrow. But for now, rest. You'll need your energy."

With that, Mr. Whitmore vanished, leaving Emma alone in the attic with the typewriter. As she slowly made her way back down to her room, her mind buzzed with the implications of what she had just agreed to. The world as she knew it had changed, and she was about to embark on a journey that would blur the lines between the living and the dead, and between fact and fiction.

## First Assignment

The following morning, Emma woke up with a lingering sense of unease. The events of the previous night felt like a strange dream, yet the antique typewriter sitting on her desk was a stark reminder that it was all too real. As she stared at it, she felt a mix of excitement and dread. How could she possibly write a story for a ghost? And what if she failed?

Before she could dwell too long on her doubts, the air in her room grew colder, and Mr. Whitmore materialized once more, his presence now familiar but still unnerving. He nodded to Emma, his expression serious.

"Good morning, Emma. I trust you've rested well," he began. "Today, we have our first task—a woman named Margaret, who passed many years ago. Her story is one of unresolved emotions, particularly toward her estranged daughter. It's a delicate matter."

Emma swallowed hard, nodding in response. "How do we... start?" she asked, her voice trembling slightly.

Mr. Whitmore gestured toward the typewriter. "Sit and place your hands on the keys. Margaret's spirit will reach out to you. Listen closely, not just to her words, but to the emotions behind them. It's your job to translate her feelings into a story that captures the essence of her life."

Emma hesitated for a moment but then moved to the typewriter, her fingers hovering above the keys. As she touched them, she felt a faint tingling sensation, as if the typewriter was coming to life under her touch. The room around her seemed to fade, and soon, she was no longer in her bedroom but in a hazy, dream-like space where she could sense another presence—Margaret.

The first thing Emma noticed was the overwhelming sadness that filled the air. It was heavy, almost suffocating, and it made her heart ache. Margaret's voice, soft and wavering, began to speak, not through words but through emotions that flooded Emma's mind.

"I was a mother, once," Margaret's thoughts whispered, laced with regret. "But I wasn't a good one. My daughter... she deserved better."

Images flashed before Emma's eyes—fragments of memories that told Margaret's story. She saw a young woman, Margaret, full of life and hope, holding her newborn daughter for the first time. But as the years passed, those hopes were replaced by bitterness and disappointment. The bond between mother and daughter frayed, strained by misunderstandings and unspoken words.

Emma's fingers moved on the typewriter, almost of their own accord, translating these emotions into words. Each keystroke felt like a piece of Margaret's soul being imprinted onto the paper. The process was draining; the sorrow and regret Margaret carried were palpable, and Emma could feel them weighing on her own heart.

Margaret's voice grew stronger as she relived her regrets. "I pushed her away. I was too proud, too stubborn to admit I was wrong. And then... it was too late."

The images shifted, showing Margaret as an older woman, alone in her home, clutching a photograph of her daughter. There was no reconciliation, no final goodbye—just years of silence and the burden of unresolved guilt.

As the story unfolded on the page, Emma realized that this was more than just writing down words. She was giving voice to a soul that had been silenced by death, allowing Margaret to express what she could not in life. The emotional weight of the task was immense, but Emma pushed through, knowing that this was her responsibility.

By the time she finished typing, Emma felt drained, both physically and emotionally. The story she had written was raw and honest, capturing Margaret's love, regret, and the longing for forgiveness that had haunted her even in death.

As Emma pulled the final sheet of paper from the typewriter, she felt the room's atmosphere shift. The sadness that had filled the space slowly dissipated, replaced by a sense of calm. Margaret's presence was no longer oppressive; instead, it felt lighter, as if a great burden had been lifted.

Mr. Whitmore, who had been watching silently, stepped forward and gently took the completed story from Emma's hands. He read through it, nodding in approval.

"Well done, Emma," he said softly. "You've done more than write a story—you've helped a soul find peace. Margaret can now move on, knowing that her feelings and regrets have been acknowledged."

Emma looked at the typewriter, her heart still heavy with the emotions she had just experienced. "This is harder than I thought," she admitted, her voice trembling.

"It is," Mr. Whitmore agreed. "But it's also a noble task. These stories, these lives—they deserve to be remembered, to be understood. And you, Emma, have the gift to make that happen."

As Mr. Whitmore spoke, Emma realized the true weight of the responsibility she had taken on. This was more than just a strange, supernatural job—it was a way to honor the lives and legacies of those who could no longer speak for themselves. She wasn't just writing stories; she was helping souls find closure, healing the wounds of the past, and ensuring that their stories would not be forgotten.

With a newfound sense of purpose, Emma nodded. "I'm ready for whatever comes next," she said, her voice steady despite the emotional toll of the day.

Mr. Whitmore smiled, a hint of pride in his ghostly eyes. "Then let us continue, my dear apprentice. There are many more stories to tell."

## Uncovering Mysteries

The days following her first assignment left Emma both exhausted and exhilarated. She had helped a lost soul find peace, but the experience had left her with more questions than answers. Each time she sat down at the typewriter, her hands hovered hesitantly over the keys, knowing that every new story could plunge her into another emotional journey.

As the weeks passed, Emma began to notice peculiar patterns in the stories she was writing. Each ghost she assisted seemed to have ties to her small town, Silverbrook. The names, places, and events mentioned in their tales began to form a tangled web of connections that spanned generations. What at first seemed like isolated stories of regret, love, and loss started to reveal a deeper, more complex history of the town—one that was not entirely reflected in its official records.

One evening, as Emma settled in for another session with the typewriter, she was visited by a spirit whose presence felt different from the others. This ghost, a middle-aged man with a somber expression, did not carry the same sense of sorrow or regret that Emma had come to expect. Instead, there was an urgency in his demeanor, a pressing need to be heard.

Emma placed her fingers on the keys, and the man's voice filled her mind, sharper and more insistent than the others.

"My name is Robert Caldwell," the spirit began. "And I have a story that needs to be told."

As Robert's story unfolded, Emma felt a chill run down her spine. He spoke of an incident that had occurred nearly fifty years ago, an event that had been carefully erased from the town's collective memory. Robert had been a witness to a crime—a murder—that had been covered up by influential figures in Silverbrook. The victim, a young woman named Lily Warren, had been silenced, her death ruled an accident, but Robert knew the truth.

Emma's fingers moved swiftly, recording every detail of Robert's account. He described how he had tried to come forward with what he knew, only to be threatened into silence by those who had something to lose. Over the years, he had watched as the true culprits rose to prominence in the town, their reputations untainted by their past sins. Now, even in death, Robert's guilt for not doing more to expose the truth weighed heavily on his soul.

As Emma typed, she realized the gravity of what she was uncovering. This was no ordinary story of unresolved feelings or unfinished business—this was a confession that had the potential to shake the foundations of her town. The people Robert implicated were not just any citizens; they were some of the most respected individuals in Silverbrook's history, names that adorned plaques and buildings.

When Emma finished writing, she sat back, staring at the pages in disbelief. The story Robert had told was chilling, and the implications were terrifying. She knew she couldn't keep this to herself, but she also understood the danger in exposing such a powerful secret.

The air in her room grew colder as Robert's presence faded, his voice now tinged with relief. "Thank you, Emma," he said softly. "You've given me a chance to make things right."

Emma nodded, though her heart raced with fear. "What do I do now?" she whispered, more to herself than to Robert.

"You must be careful," Mr. Whitmore's voice interrupted her thoughts. He materialized beside her, his expression grave. "There are those who would go to great lengths to keep this buried. You've uncovered something dangerous, Emma. But you also have the power to bring justice."

Emma looked at Mr. Whitmore, her mind racing. "How can I expose this? Who would believe me?"

Mr. Whitmore's gaze softened, and he placed a ghostly hand on her shoulder. "The truth has a way of coming to light, even in the darkest of places. But you must be strategic. Find allies, people you can trust. Use the stories you write to guide them. The living have a right to know what has been hidden for so long."

Emma's thoughts turned to the people in her life—her family, her friends, her teachers. Who could she trust with something so monumental? And what would happen if she brought this story into the open? The idea of confronting those responsible filled her with dread, but she knew she couldn't walk away from this.

Over the next few days, Emma found herself consumed by Robert's story. She visited the local library, poring over old newspaper archives, searching for any mention of Lily Warren or the incident Robert had described. To her frustration, there was almost nothing—a small obituary for Lily, citing a tragic accident, and a few mentions of the people Robert had accused, all in glowing terms.

It was as if the entire town had conspired to forget what had happened. But Emma couldn't forget. She couldn't ignore the plea for justice that had been entrusted to her.

As she delved deeper, Emma started to notice subtle hints in other stories she had written, clues that linked back to Robert's tale. It was as if the ghosts were guiding her, pointing her toward the truth. The more she uncovered, the more she realized that this was no isolated incident. The town's history was riddled with secrets, hidden beneath a veneer of respectability.

Emma knew she was in over her head, but she couldn't stop now. She had been given a responsibility—a mission—to bring these buried truths to light. But the closer she got to the heart of the mystery, the more dangerous it became. Whispers of her investigation began to spread, and she felt the weight of unseen eyes watching her, waiting for her next move.

The typewriter, once a tool of discovery and connection, now felt like a burden—a conduit for voices that demanded justice, even if it put Emma at risk. But she couldn't turn back. She had a story to tell, and she would see it through, no matter the cost.

## Weight of Legacy

Emma sat at her desk, staring at the latest manuscript she had completed. The typewriter keys were silent now, but the echoes of the stories she had written seemed to linger in the air, heavy and oppressive. Each page bore the weight of a life once lived, a story that had been hidden, and a legacy that was now unearthed for the world to see. The more she delved into the lives of the dead, the more she felt the burden of their unfinished business pressing down on her shoulders.

At first, the work had been exhilarating. The thrill of discovery, the satisfaction of helping spirits find peace, and the sense of purpose that came with her new role had driven her forward. But as the stories piled up, so did the emotional toll. Each spirit's story carried its own pain, its own unresolved feelings, and its own impact on the living world.

The manuscript in front of her was one of the most difficult she had written yet. It told the story of a man named Samuel, who had died suddenly in a car accident, leaving behind a young family. His spirit had been restless, consumed by guilt and regret for not being able to provide for his wife and children after his death. He had asked Emma to write a letter to his family, expressing his love and apologizing for the things he had left unfinished.

As she typed out Samuel's heartfelt words, Emma could feel the depth of his sorrow and the love he had for his family. She had sent the letter to his widow, hoping it would bring her some measure of comfort. But instead of closure, the letter had reopened old wounds. Samuel's widow, who had spent years trying to move on from her grief, was suddenly confronted with the past all over again. The pain of losing her husband was fresh once more, and Emma couldn't help but feel responsible.

Emma began to wonder if every story deserved to be told. Was it right to dredge up the past, even if it meant causing pain to those still living? The spirits she helped seemed to find peace through her writing, but what about the people they left behind? Could the truth really set them free, or was it sometimes better to let sleeping dogs lie?

She thought back to Margaret, the ghost from her first assignment. Margaret's story had brought healing to her estranged daughter, who had found solace in knowing that her mother had loved her, despite their troubled relationship. But not every story had such a happy ending.

Some brought more harm than good, and Emma was beginning to see that her role as a ghostwriter was far more complex than she had imagined.

As the weeks passed, the weight of her work began to take its toll. Emma found herself struggling to sleep, her mind racing with the stories she had written and the ones she had yet to uncover. She started to withdraw from her friends and family, consumed by the ghosts who demanded her attention. The line between the living and the dead grew increasingly blurred, and Emma felt like she was caught in the middle, unsure of where she belonged.

One afternoon, after finishing yet another emotionally charged story, Emma decided to take a break. She walked through the quiet streets of Silverbrook, hoping the fresh air would clear her mind. But everywhere she looked, she saw reminders of the stories she had uncovered—an old church where a wedding had taken place, a park where children once played, a dilapidated building that had once been a thriving business. The town was alive with history, and Emma could feel the weight of its legacy pressing down on her.

As she wandered, lost in thought, she found herself standing in front of the town's cemetery. The iron gates creaked as she pushed them open, and she slowly made her way through the rows of gravestones. She read the names and dates etched into the stone, wondering about the lives these people had lived and the stories they had left behind.

In the distance, she saw a figure standing by a grave. It was Mr. Whitmore, his ghostly form barely visible in the fading light. He looked up as she approached, his expression unreadable.

"You're carrying a heavy burden, Emma," he said softly. "I can see it in your eyes."

Emma nodded, feeling the weight of his words. "I didn't realize how hard this would be," she admitted. "I thought I was helping people, but now I'm not so sure. Some of these stories… they're just too painful."

Mr. Whitmore nodded, his gaze distant. "The truth is a double-edged sword, my dear. It can bring closure, but it can also cause pain. Every story you write has consequences, and not all of them are pleasant."

Emma sighed, feeling a knot of guilt in her chest. "How do I know if I'm doing the right thing? What if I'm just making things worse?"

"There's no easy answer," Mr. Whitmore replied. "But you must remember that you are giving a voice to those who can no longer speak for themselves. You are honoring their legacy, even if it's difficult. The living may struggle with the truth, but it is their right to know."

Emma looked down at the ground, her thoughts swirling. "But what about the people who are hurt by these stories? What about their pain?"

"Pain is a part of life, Emma," Mr. Whitmore said gently. "We cannot shield ourselves from it, nor can we shield others. But through pain, we grow. We learn. We find strength we didn't know we had. The stories you write may cause pain, but they also offer a chance for healing—for both the living and the dead."

Emma nodded, taking in his words. She knew he was right, but it didn't make the burden any easier to bear. As she looked out over the cemetery, she felt a renewed sense of responsibility. The stories she wrote were not just about the past—they were about the present and the future as well. They were about legacy, about what we leave behind for those who come after us.

She turned to Mr. Whitmore, her resolve hardening. "I'll keep writing," she said firmly. "But I'll be careful. I'll make sure that the stories I tell are worth the consequences."

Mr. Whitmore smiled, a glimmer of pride in his eyes. "That's all any of us can do, Emma. Keep writing, keep telling the truth, and trust that you are making a difference."

As Emma left the cemetery that day, she felt a renewed sense of purpose. The weight of her work was still heavy, but it was a burden she was willing to bear. She would continue to be a ghostwriter, not just for the dead, but for the living as well. And in doing so, she would honor the legacies of those who had come before her, while also forging her own.

## Glimpse of the Afterlife

Emma's latest assignment is proving to be the most challenging yet. She has been tasked with writing the story of a young woman named Clara, whose life was cut short by a tragic accident. Clara's ghost is filled with sorrow and regret, and her fragmented memories are difficult for Emma to piece together. Each night, Emma finds herself wrestling with the emotional weight of Clara's story, feeling the strain of unspoken grief and unresolved pain.

One evening, as Emma works late into the night, the weight of Clara's sorrow seems to seep through the walls of the attic. Exhaustion overtakes her, and she falls asleep at the typewriter, her fingers still poised over the keys.

In her sleep, Emma finds herself in a dreamlike state, transported to an ethereal realm that defies the constraints of reality. She stands at the edge of a vast, shimmering lake, its surface reflecting an ever-changing sky of vibrant hues—pinks, blues, and purples blending in a mesmerizing dance. The air is thick with mist, and the sounds of soft, melancholic music drift through the fog.

As Emma steps forward, she notices that the mist forms shifting shapes and figures, representing the souls that linger in this space. She sees spirits floating gracefully, their forms translucent and glowing with a soft light. They move in patterns that suggest a kind of dance, a gentle but sorrowful ballet of memories and emotions.

Among the spirits, Emma recognizes several from her previous assignments: Margaret, whose estranged daughter now holds her hand; Mr. Fletcher, still gazing longingly at the distant figure of his lost love. Each spirit seems to emanate a blend of relief and residual sorrow, a mixture of peace and unfinished business.

Emma is drawn towards a particularly intense presence, feeling a deep, pulling emotion that resonates with Clara's story. She sees Clara's ghost standing by the lake's edge, her figure faint and flickering like a candle in the wind.

Clara gazes into the water, where the reflection of her lost moments ripples and fades.

Suddenly, a gentle, yet commanding voice echoes through the mist. The voice speaks of the afterlife as a place of both beauty and torment—a realm where unresolved emotions can trap souls, preventing them from moving on. It tells Emma that the afterlife is not a static destination but a dynamic space where the balance of emotions can affect the spirits' ability to find peace.

Emma watches as Clara's reflection shifts into a myriad of images—moments of joy, sorrow, and the tragic accident that ended her life. The vision is overwhelming, a powerful reminder of the gravity of Emma's work. Each story she writes not only helps spirits find closure but also has the potential to either free or further bind them to their earthly regrets.

The mist starts to close in around Emma, the figures becoming more indistinct as if the afterlife itself is receding from her reach. The surreal experience leaves her feeling both enlightened and daunted. She awakens in her attic, the typewriter quiet and still before her, her heart racing from the intensity of the vision.

Emma realizes that her role as a ghostwriter is more significant than she had ever imagined. It's not just about telling stories; it's about navigating the complex interplay of emotions that define both the living and the dead. She understands now that her words have the power to shape destinies, and with this realization comes a renewed sense of responsibility and purpose. Emma is more determined than ever to honor the spirits' stories and help them find the peace they seek, aware of the delicate balance she must maintain between the realms of the living and the dead.

## The Living and the Dead

Emma's life has become a delicate balancing act. As she continues her apprenticeship with Mr. Whitmore, she is increasingly faced with the reactions of the living relatives to the stories she writes for the spirits. Her involvement in the world of the dead has brought a new layer of complexity to her interactions with the living.

One evening, Emma receives an urgent request from Mr. Whitmore. The spirit of Henry, a man who had suffered a tragic end, has been particularly restless. His story is one of regret and unresolved conflict with his estranged brother, David. Emma completes the story with the utmost care, capturing Henry's feelings of remorse and his desperate wish for reconciliation.

Upon delivering the story to David, Emma encounters resistance. David is a skeptical man who has spent years trying to move past his troubled relationship with his brother. He dismisses the story as a fabrication, accusing Emma of exploiting his family's pain for personal gain. His anger is palpable, and he refuses to accept the truth of Henry's message.

As days pass, Emma starts to experience disturbances at home. The same restless spirit that she had written about begins to manifest in her own life. At first, it's small things—a book falling off a shelf, cold spots in the attic— but soon the manifestations become more unsettling: whispers in the dark, shadows moving in the corners of her vision, and a pervasive sense of unease that never quite fades.

One night, as Emma struggles to sleep, the spirit of Henry appears in her room. He is not menacing, but his sadness is overwhelming. Emma realizes that Henry's unrest is now affecting her directly because his story has not been accepted by those he hoped to reach. The spirit's inability to find peace is causing a ripple effect, impacting both the living and the dead.

Determined to resolve the situation, Emma decides to confront David directly. She arranges a meeting with him and comes prepared with evidence—photographs, letters, and historical documents that corroborate the details in Henry's story. Emma also shares her own experiences with Henry's spirit, including the disturbances she has faced.

During their meeting, Emma speaks with genuine emotion, detailing how Henry's story has affected her and the importance of acknowledging the past to find closure. David, initially resistant, is moved by Emma's sincerity and the tangible proof she presents. Though still skeptical, he begins to soften and reluctantly agrees to reconsider the validity of the story.

Emma works with David to reconstruct his relationship with his late brother. Together, they visit places significant to Henry's life and reflect on their shared memories. This process helps David come to terms with his own grief and allows him to acknowledge the truth in Henry's story.

As David makes peace with the past, the disturbances in Emma's home gradually cease. Henry's spirit appears one last time to thank Emma, his presence now peaceful and serene. Emma is relieved to see the spirit finally find the closure he sought.

Through this experience, Emma learns the intricate connections between the living and the dead. She realizes that her role as a ghostwriter is not only to craft stories but also to bridge the gap between these two worlds. The living's acceptance and understanding of the past play a crucial role in allowing the dead to move on, and Emma's work has a profound impact on both realms.

This chapter highlights the challenges Emma faces as she navigates the complex dynamics of her work, showcasing the importance of empathy and communication in resolving both the spirits' and the living's emotional conflicts. Emma's journey through this chapter deepens her understanding of the delicate balance required to help both the dead and the living find peace.

## Final Story

Emma's time with Mr. Whitmore has been transformative, a journey through the ethereal world of ghosts and the stories they leave behind. Yet, as they sit together one evening in the quiet of the attic, Mr. Whitmore's usually serene demeanor carries an air of finality. His translucent form seems to flicker with a mixture of sadness and relief.

"Emma," Mr. Whitmore begins, his voice carrying a weight that makes Emma's heart sink. "There's one last story I need you to write."

Emma's eyes widen with concern. "What do you mean, Mr. Whitmore? You've been my mentor, my guide. I can't imagine doing this without you."

Mr. Whitmore's ghostly presence seems to grow more solid, as if he's mustering the last of his strength. "It's my own story. I've been helping spirits find closure, but I've neglected my own unfinished business. It's time for you to help me complete it."

The request is both daunting and poignant. Emma takes a deep breath and nods, determined to honor the mentor who has guided her through the complexities of ghostwriting.

The process begins with Emma diving into Mr. Whitmore's past, sifting through his memories and the fragments of his life that linger in the attic. She learns that Mr. Whitmore was once a celebrated writer who specialized in capturing the voices of the dead. His work was revered, but his personal life was marked by regret and sorrow. His estranged relationship with his daughter, who he was never able to reconcile with before his death, is the root of his lingering unrest.

Emma reads through Mr. Whitmore's old letters and diaries, uncovering the story of a man who dedicated his life to others but failed to mend the most important relationships in his own life. She discovers the pain and isolation Mr. Whitmore felt, which kept him bound to the mortal realm. His regrets are palpable, and Emma feels the weight of his unfulfilled desires and unresolved issues as she writes.

The narrative of Mr. Whitmore's life unfolds like a somber tapestry, woven with threads of ambition, lost love, and personal failures. Emma writes about his early successes, his rise to prominence, and the eventual unraveling of his personal life. She captures his struggles with fame, his regrets over missed opportunities with his daughter, and the deep sense of guilt that has haunted him.

Throughout the writing process, Emma finds herself emotionally entwined with Mr. Whitmore's story. The task becomes increasingly difficult as she confronts the depth of his sorrow and the personal impact his regrets have had on him. She reflects on her own life and the lessons Mr. Whitmore has imparted, grappling with her feelings of impending loss.

As Emma nears the end of writing Mr. Whitmore's story, she feels a profound sense of grief and accomplishment. She has poured her heart into capturing the essence of a man who has become a mentor and friend. The final draft is a poignant portrayal of Mr. Whitmore's life—a testament to his contributions and his shortcomings.

One quiet evening, Emma presents the finished manuscript to Mr. Whitmore. His ghostly figure appears both relieved and wistful as he reads through the pages. The story is a reflection of his life and his regrets, rendered with the empathy and skill Emma has developed during her apprenticeship.

"This is more than I could have hoped for," Mr. Whitmore says softly, his voice tinged with emotion. "You've given my story the voice it needed. I can finally move on."

As Mr. Whitmore's spirit begins to fade, Emma feels a deep sense of loss but also a profound sense of gratitude.

She has completed her mentor's final request and has gained invaluable insights into the nature of legacy and closure.

The chapter closes with Emma standing alone in the attic, holding the last pages of Mr. Whitmore's story. The space feels quieter, more peaceful, as if the weight of the past has been lifted. Emma reflects on the impact Mr. Whitmore's mentorship has had on her life and the lessons she has learned about storytelling, empathy, and the human condition.

## Moving On

The attic is quiet in the aftermath of Mr. Whitmore's departure, the typewriter's keys resting still for the first time in weeks. Emma sits alone amidst the manuscripts and notes that have become so familiar to her. The room feels both emptier and fuller—empty of Mr. Whitmore's guiding presence but filled with the weight of the lessons she has learned and the stories she has written.

Emma holds the final manuscript of Mr. Whitmore's story, its pages now bound and complete. She feels a mixture of sadness and satisfaction as she reflects on the journey she has undertaken. The experience of helping Mr. Whitmore find peace has left an indelible mark on her, and she understands the gravity of what she has accomplished.

In the quiet moments following Mr. Whitmore's departure, Emma feels a profound sense of loss. He was not just a mentor but a guiding force in her life, and his absence is palpable. Yet, this loss is tempered by the knowledge that he has finally found the closure he sought. Emma is left with the memory of his gratitude and the impact his story had on her own perspective.

Emma begins to sift through the remaining papers and personal effects in the attic. She finds fragments of other stories—unfinished tales of spirits who, like Mr. Whitmore, have left behind pieces of their lives waiting to be told. These papers are a testament to the ongoing nature of her mentor's work and the many souls still seeking resolution.

As she reads through these fragments, Emma feels a renewed sense of purpose. The stories she encounters are filled with the same emotional depth and complexity that Mr. Whitmore's story had. She realizes that her journey is far from over. The skills she has developed and the insights she has gained are tools she can use to continue Mr. Whitmore's legacy.

Determined to honor her mentor's memory and the spirits she has helped, Emma makes the decision to continue the work. She sets up a small office in the attic, transforming it into a space dedicated to the craft of ghostwriting. The typewriter, now imbued with the memories of countless stories, is placed prominently on her desk, ready for the stories yet to be told.

Emma begins to work on the next story, her approach marked by a newfound sense of confidence and empathy. She understands the delicate balance required to honor both the living and the dead through her writing. Her work is no longer just about capturing the past but about bridging the gap between the realms of life and death.

As Emma writes, she reflects on the lessons she has learned from Mr. Whitmore and the spirits she has encountered. She understands now that storytelling is not just a means of preserving memories but a powerful tool for healing and connection. The stories she writes are not merely accounts of the past; they are vehicles for understanding, reconciliation, and peace.

One evening, as Emma looks out the attic window, she sees the first stars of the evening sky. The tranquility of the scene mirrors the peace she feels within herself. She knows that she is on the right path, continuing a legacy of compassion and understanding that transcends the boundaries of life and death.

The chapter closes with Emma starting a new manuscript, her heart filled with both hope and resolve. She is ready to face the challenges ahead, knowing that her work as a ghostwriter is not just about the dead but about creating a bridge between worlds, offering solace to those who need it, and enriching her own understanding of life and the stories that define it.

## The Next Chapter

The attic is now a vibrant workspace, transformed by Emma's dedication and the countless stories that have been written within its walls. The once dusty room is organized and welcoming, with shelves lined with manuscripts and a cozy reading nook by the window where Emma often reflects on her work. The typewriter, polished and prominent, stands as a symbol of her continued journey and the stories still waiting to be told.

Emma has embraced her role as a ghostwriter with newfound vigor. Her days are filled with a blend of the mundane and the extraordinary—balancing her everyday life with the extraordinary task of helping spirits find closure. Her interactions with the living world have become more profound, and she has formed a deeper appreciation for the connections she has with those around her.

One afternoon, Emma receives a letter from an old friend, inviting her to a local community event. Despite her initial hesitation, she decides to attend, finding that her experiences have given her a fresh perspective on her relationships and interactions with others. At the event, she reconnects with friends and family, sharing snippets of her journey without revealing the full extent of her ghostwriting work. Her ability to listen and empathize makes her a valued presence among her peers, demonstrating how her unique experiences have enriched her understanding of human emotions.

Back in the attic, Emma begins working on a new project—a book of collected stories from the spirits she has helped. The book will be a tribute to their lives and a way to share their messages with the world. Each chapter is dedicated to a different spirit, capturing their unique voices and the impact their stories have had on Emma and those they left behind. The project becomes a labor of love, intertwining her personal growth with the legacies of the spirits she has written for.

One evening, as Emma types away, the typewriter begins to move on its own, a subtle reminder of the supernatural connection that still exists. The feeling is both comforting and exhilarating, a sign that her role in bridging the worlds of the living and the dead is far from over. The typewriter's rhythmic clacking becomes a soothing background noise as she writes, reinforcing the bond between her and the spirits she continues to help.

Emma also starts to seek out new spirits who may need her assistance. She develops a network of local historians, mediumists, and others who are in touch with the spiritual realm. Through these connections, she learns about new cases and begins to tackle the stories of spirits whose unresolved issues have affected their loved ones.

Her work is not without its challenges. Each new story brings its own set of emotional complexities, and Emma must navigate these with care and sensitivity. She has learned to approach each case with a balance of empathy and professionalism, recognizing the impact her writing can have on both the deceased and the living.

As the seasons change, Emma reflects on her journey and the growth she has experienced. She understands that her role as a ghostwriter is a continual one—each story she writes not only helps the spirits find peace but also shapes her own path. The typewriter, a constant companion, reminds her of the stories yet to be told and the lives she has touched.

The chapter concludes with Emma sitting by the attic window, looking out at the night sky. The stars twinkle above, and she feels a deep sense of fulfillment. She knows that her work is far from over and that every story she writes is another step in her journey. Emma is ready to face the future with confidence, knowing that she is part of a larger narrative that transcends the boundaries of life and death.

* * * *

# CODE OF STARS

## Strange Alignment

Sixteen-year-old Maya had always found solace in the night sky. While other teens spent their evenings on social media or hanging out with friends, Maya's refuge was her backyard observatory—a simple setup with her trusty telescope, a few star charts, and a notebook filled with observations. For as long as she could remember, the stars had been her companions, twinkling beacons of light in the vast darkness, each one a mystery waiting to be unraveled.

One evening, as she adjusted the focus on her telescope, something caught her eye. A cluster of stars, usually scattered across the sky in a seemingly random pattern, appeared to be aligning. The stars shifted ever so slightly, forming a distinct, intricate pattern that Maya had never seen before. She leaned closer, her breath catching in her throat. This wasn't just a coincidence—this was something deliberate, something intentional.

Maya quickly grabbed her notebook, her heart pounding with excitement and curiosity. She sketched the pattern as best as she could, tracing the lines between the stars, noting their brightness and position in the sky. The pattern resembled an ancient symbol, though Maya couldn't quite place it. She flipped through her star charts, but nothing matched what she had just seen.

Over the next few nights, Maya became obsessed with the alignment. She spent hours under the stars, observing the subtle movements of the celestial bodies. The pattern seemed to evolve, shifting slightly each night, as if the stars were engaged in a slow, deliberate dance. The more she observed, the more certain she became—these stars were communicating with each other. But why? And what were they trying to say?

Maya's curiosity deepened, and she began to notice something even stranger. As she focused on the stars, she felt an odd connection, as if she could almost sense their movements before they happened. It was as if the pattern was speaking to her, revealing a code that only she could understand. She started deciphering the shifts in the alignment, trying to decode the celestial messages hidden within.

Her nights were filled with wonder and mystery as she immersed herself in the task. She felt a pull toward the stars that she couldn't explain, a sense that something bigger was at play, something that she was meant to discover. The more she studied the alignment, the more she felt like she was on the verge of uncovering a secret that had been hidden for eons.

Maya's life during the day began to blur with her nighttime explorations. At school, she found herself daydreaming about the stars, sketching patterns in the margins of her notebooks. Her friends noticed the change in her, but Maya brushed off their concerns, too engrossed in the cosmic mystery to care. Every evening, as soon as the sun dipped below the horizon, she would rush to her telescope, eager to see how the stars had moved.

The pattern grew more complex, each night revealing new connections and symbols. Maya's notebook filled with cryptic sketches and notes, each page a testament to the hours she spent decoding the celestial messages. She felt like a cosmic detective, piecing together a puzzle that spanned the universe.

One night, as she stared up at the sky, a sudden realization struck her—the stars weren't just communicating with each other. They were communicating with her. The pattern wasn't just a random alignment; it was a code, a message meant for someone who could decipher it. And somehow, impossibly, Maya knew that she was that someone.

Her heart raced as the implications of this dawned on her. She was being called upon by the stars, drawn into a mystery that transcended time and space. The alignment wasn't just a celestial event—it was the beginning of something extraordinary, a journey that would take her far beyond the familiar confines of her backyard observatory.

With a mixture of excitement and trepidation, Maya vowed to uncover the secrets of the stars. She didn't know where this journey would lead her, but one thing was certain: her life was about to change forever.

As she looked up at the sky that night, the stars seemed to twinkle brighter, as if acknowledging her newfound resolve. The pattern was clear now, the message unmistakable—Maya was meant to follow the code, to unravel the mysteries of the cosmos and discover the truth hidden in the stars.

And so, with her telescope pointed toward the heavens and her notebook open on her lap, Maya embarked on her journey into the unknown, ready to decode the language of the stars and uncover the secrets they held.

## First Contact

The discovery of the celestial pattern consumed Maya's every waking moment. Each night, she would return to her telescope, her heart racing with anticipation as she charted the stars' shifting positions. The more she decoded, the more intricate and interconnected the pattern became. It was as if the stars were telling a story, one that only she could understand. But what that story was, she had yet to uncover.

One particularly clear night, as Maya adjusted her telescope, she noticed something unusual. The stars within the pattern were glowing brighter than usual, their light pulsating in rhythmic intervals. It was as if they were trying to communicate something urgent, something that demanded her immediate attention. She quickly scribbled down the sequence in her notebook, trying to make sense of the new development.

As she stared at the sky, the pattern suddenly seemed to come alive, the stars vibrating with an intensity that sent chills down her spine. Then, to her astonishment, the light from the stars began to coalesce, forming a glowing, ethereal figure right before her eyes. Maya's breath caught in her throat as she watched the figure take shape, its outline shimmering with a soft, otherworldly light.

The figure was tall and graceful, with flowing robes that seemed to be made of stardust. Its eyes, like twin galaxies, held a depth that both mesmerized and intimidated Maya. For a moment, she could only stare in stunned silence, unable to process what was happening. This wasn't just a pattern in the sky—this was something far more profound.

"Do not be afraid," the figure spoke, its voice like the whisper of the wind, both gentle and commanding. "I am Astra, a being of the stars. You have been chosen, Maya."

Maya's heart pounded in her chest, her mind racing with questions. "Chosen? Chosen for what?"

Astra's gaze softened as it regarded her. "You have a unique gift, Maya. The stars have been speaking to you, and you have the ability to understand their language. The pattern you have been decoding is not just a random alignment—it is a message, a call for help."

"A call for help?" Maya echoed, her voice tinged with disbelief. "From who? Why me?"

"The stars are alive, Maya. They are ancient, wise beings who have watched over the universe for eons," Astra explained. "But they are not invincible. A cosmic conflict has been brewing, one that threatens the very fabric of the universe. The stars have chosen you to help resolve this conflict, for it is one that could affect not only the stars but also your world."

Maya's mind reeled with the enormity of what Astra was saying. The stars were alive? A cosmic conflict that could impact Earth? It was almost too much to comprehend. But as she looked into Astra's eyes, she could sense the truth in the celestial being's words.

"But… how can I help?" Maya asked, her voice trembling slightly. "I'm just a teenager. I don't know anything about cosmic conflicts or celestial beings."

Astra smiled, a serene and knowing expression. "You are more capable than you realize, Maya. The stars have seen something in you—something rare and powerful. You have the ability to decode their messages, to understand the cosmic language that few others can. This conflict is not just a battle of might; it is a battle of understanding, of communication. And you are the key."

Maya felt a mix of fear and determination welling up inside her. The idea of being involved in something so vast and incomprehensible was daunting, but at the same time, she couldn't deny the thrill of it. The stars had been her companions for as long as she could remember, and now they were calling on her for help.

"What do I need to do?" she asked, her voice steadying as she made her decision.

Astra's form seemed to glow brighter, as if pleased by her resolve. "You must continue decoding the pattern, but you must also prepare yourself for what lies ahead. There are forces at play that seek to disrupt the harmony of the cosmos, and they will not be easily defeated. But you will not be alone. The stars will guide you, and I will be here to help you understand their messages."

Maya nodded, feeling a strange sense of calm wash over her. The path ahead was uncertain, and the stakes were higher than she had ever imagined. But she knew she couldn't turn back now. The stars had chosen her for a reason, and she was determined to see this journey through.

As Astra began to fade, the celestial being left Maya with one final message. "Remember, Maya, the stars are not just lights in the sky. They are alive, and they are counting on you. The code you are decoding is the key to saving not just them, but your world as well."

With that, Astra disappeared, leaving Maya alone with her thoughts and the vast, starry sky above her. The weight of her newfound responsibility settled on her shoulders, but she felt more determined than ever. The stars had entrusted her with their secrets, and she would not let them down

As she looked up at the night sky, the pattern of stars seemed to twinkle in affirmation, as if acknowledging her commitment. With renewed purpose, Maya returned to her telescope, ready to continue decoding the celestial code and uncover the mysteries that lay within.

This was only the beginning, and Maya knew that her journey into the cosmos would take her to places she had never imagined, both in the stars and within herself.

## Cosmic Conflict Unveiled

After her first encounter with Astra, Maya found herself filled with a mixture of excitement and trepidation. The stars, once just distant lights in the night sky, had taken on a new significance. They were alive, conscious, and embroiled in a conflict that could have repercussions for the entire universe—including Earth.

A few nights later, as Maya was once again studying the star pattern, Astra appeared before her, radiating the same gentle light as before. This time, however, there was an urgency in Astra's presence that Maya hadn't noticed before.

"Maya," Astra began, "it is time for you to see the full scope of what we are facing. The stars are not merely observing the universe; they are active participants in a struggle that could determine the fate of countless worlds."

Maya swallowed, her heart racing. "What do you mean? What kind of struggle?"

Astra extended a hand toward Maya, who hesitated only for a moment before taking it. Instantly, she felt a surge of energy, and the world around her dissolved into a swirl of light and stars. She felt weightless, as though she were floating through space itself, surrounded by the vastness of the cosmos. It was both exhilarating and terrifying.

As the swirling lights began to settle, Maya found herself standing on what seemed to be a platform of stardust, suspended in the middle of a cosmic expanse. Around her, stars blazed with a brilliance she had never seen before. Some were clustered together, their light pulsating in harmonious waves, while others flickered erratically, their energy chaotic and unstable.

"These are the factions," Astra explained, gesturing to the stars. "On one side, you have the stars who seek to maintain the balance of the universe. They understand that harmony is essential to the survival of all life, that each star and planet plays a role in the grand design of existence."

Maya gazed at the stars clustered together, their light steady and rhythmic. She could feel their unity, their shared purpose, like the beat of a collective heart.

"But on the other side," Astra continued, her voice darkening, "there are those who desire control. They seek to impose their will on the cosmos, to bend the universe to their vision of order. They believe that power is the ultimate goal, and they are willing to disrupt the balance to achieve it."

Maya turned to look at the flickering stars, their light sharp and erratic. There was a sense of discord among them, a restlessness that set them apart from the others. It was as if they were on the verge of exploding, their energy unstable and unpredictable.

"This conflict has been brewing for eons," Astra said, her gaze distant. "The stars that seek control have grown more powerful, and their influence is spreading. If they succeed, the consequences will be felt across the universe—including on Earth."

Maya felt a chill run down her spine. The idea that this cosmic struggle could affect her own world was frightening. But as she stood there, surrounded by the stars, she began to see the parallels between this cosmic conflict and the issues she recognized from Earth. Power struggles, division, the desire to control—these were not just cosmic issues, but human ones as well.

"The celestial code you've been deciphering," Astra continued, "is a cry for help from the stars caught in the middle of this conflict. They are the ones who understand the importance of balance but lack the power to resist the factions that seek control. They are reaching out to you, Maya, because they believe you can help."

"But how can I help?" Maya asked, her voice tinged with doubt. "I'm just one person. How can I make a difference in something so vast?"

Astra turned to her, her gaze intense but filled with compassion. "You have a gift, Maya. The ability to understand the celestial language is rare, even among the stars. With this gift, you can bridge the gap between the factions, find the hidden meanings in their messages, and help restore the balance. You are more important to this struggle than you realize."

Maya took a deep breath, trying to process everything she was being told. The responsibility felt enormous, almost overwhelming. But she also felt a sense of purpose growing within her. The stars had chosen her, and she couldn't let them down.

"What do I need to do?" she asked, her voice steadying with resolve.

"You must continue to decode the celestial messages," Astra instructed. "But you must also be prepared to act. The factions will not give up their power easily, and there will be challenges ahead. But remember, you are not alone. The stars who seek balance are with you, and I will guide you as best I can."

Maya nodded, determination hardening in her chest. She knew the road ahead would be difficult, but she was ready to face it. The stars had entrusted her with their secrets, and she would do everything in her power to help them.

As Astra began to fade, Maya felt the cosmic expanse around her begin to dissolve. The stars' light dimmed, and soon she found herself back in her room, standing beside her telescope. The night sky outside her window was calm, the stars twinkling innocently as if nothing had changed.

But Maya knew better. The universe was in turmoil, and she was now a part of the struggle to save it.

With renewed determination, Maya returned to her desk, where her notebook lay open, filled with the celestial code she had been working on. The patterns seemed clearer now, the messages more urgent. As she picked up her pen and began to write, she felt a sense of purpose guiding her hand.

The conflict had been unveiled, and Maya was ready to face whatever challenges lay ahead. The stars were counting on her, and she would not let them down.

## World in Peril

As Maya delves deeper into the celestial code, she begins to notice strange occurrences on Earth that seem to mirror the cosmic conflict she has been unraveling. Unusual weather patterns, sudden earthquakes, and inexplicable shifts in the natural world start to emerge, each seemingly linked to the turmoil among the stars. The auroras, once beautiful displays of light, become ominous, their colors more vivid and intense than ever before, as if the skies themselves are crying out in distress.

Maya finds herself overwhelmed by the gravity of the situation. The code, once a fascinating puzzle, now feels like a ticking time bomb, with the potential to unravel both the cosmos and her own world. The stars, once distant and serene, now appear as watchful, desperate beings whose very existence depends on her ability to decipher their messages. The weight of her responsibility presses down on her, and she begins to struggle with doubt and fear.

At school, Maya's friends and teachers notice her growing anxiety, but she can't confide in them—how could they possibly understand? Her grades slip, and she becomes increasingly isolated, spending sleepless nights poring over the star charts and celestial maps that now dominate her room. The once comforting glow of the stars through her telescope now feels like a constant reminder of the looming crisis.

As the natural disasters intensify, news reports flood in about cities ravaged by floods, volcanic eruptions, and other inexplicable phenomena. Scientists and governments are baffled, unable to explain the sudden upheaval. Maya realizes that the celestial conflict is spilling over into the earthly realm, and the longer she takes to decode the messages, the more devastating the consequences will be.

Astra appears to Maya more frequently, guiding her through the complexities of the code and offering cryptic advice. "The stars are not merely distant lights," Astra tells her one evening, "they are woven into the very fabric of existence. What happens to them, happens to you." Maya begins to understand that the connection between the cosmos and Earth is deeper than she ever imagined, and her role in this conflict is not just to decipher the code, but to help restore the balance that has been lost.

In the midst of her struggles, Maya starts to feel a growing bond with the stars. They are no longer just distant entities in the night sky—they are her allies, her companions in this cosmic battle. Yet, with this connection comes an even greater sense of responsibility. She realizes that if she fails, it's not just the stars that will suffer, but the entire world.

As the chapter ends, Maya faces a pivotal moment: she must decide whether to continue shouldering this immense burden alone or seek help from those who care about her. The fate of both worlds depends on her next move, and time is running out.

## Mediator

Maya's newfound role as the interpreter of the celestial code thrusts her into a position she never expected: a mediator between the warring star factions. The night sky, once a place of wonder, now feels like a battleground where ancient beings vie for control, their conflicts resonating across the universe. As the only one who can understand the code, Maya becomes the key to resolving the tension that threatens both the cosmos and Earth.

Astra guides Maya to a secluded spot in the mountains, away from the chaos of the world below. Here, the stars shine brighter and clearer, and the celestial code pulses with a life of its own. It is in this place that Maya meets representatives from both factions—the Luminaries, who seek to preserve the balance of the universe, and the Umbra, who desire change and dominance, believing that the universe must evolve, even if it means conflict and destruction.

The Luminaries are beings of light, their forms shifting and shimmering with every word they speak. They represent the stars that have long maintained order, guiding civilizations and maintaining the delicate equilibrium of the cosmos. The Umbra, on the other hand, are darker, more enigmatic figures, embodying the stars that have grown tired of the status quo and wish to see the universe reborn, even if it means destruction.

Maya listens as both sides present their grievances. The Luminaries speak of the importance of stability, of how their guidance has allowed life to flourish across countless worlds. The Umbra argue that stagnation leads to decay, and that without change, the universe will wither and die. As Maya listens, she realizes that neither side is entirely right or wrong; both have valid points, and the conflict is rooted in a complex history of misunderstandings and unmet needs.

Astra encourages Maya to speak, to use her understanding of both the celestial code and the human condition to find common ground. At first, Maya is hesitant—how can a sixteen-year-old girl mediate a conflict that spans eons? But as she begins to speak, she finds that her unique perspective, informed by her experiences on Earth, allows her to see things the celestial beings cannot.

Maya proposes a series of compromises, suggesting that the Luminaries and the Umbra work together to create a new balance—one that allows for change and growth, but without the destruction that the Umbra seek. She emphasizes the importance of understanding each other's fears and desires, and the need for both stability and evolution in the cosmos. As she speaks, the celestial code responds, its patterns shifting and changing in ways that reflect the possibilities of peace.

The mediation process is not easy. Both sides are deeply entrenched in their positions, and there are moments when it seems the talks will break down entirely. The Luminaries fear losing control, while the Umbra are reluctant to compromise on their vision of a new universe. Maya must navigate these tensions carefully, using her knowledge of the code to propose solutions that respect the needs of both sides.

As the days pass, the first signs of progress begin to emerge. The Luminaries agree to allow for certain changes, acknowledging that the universe must adapt to survive. The Umbra, in turn, agree to temper their more destructive impulses, recognizing the value of preserving what is already good in the universe. It is a delicate balance, but one that seems achievable.

Maya's role as a mediator takes a toll on her. The weight of the universe rests on her shoulders, and the constant negotiations drain her physically and emotionally. Yet, she also feels a sense of purpose like never before. She is not just a passive observer in the cosmos—she is an active participant, shaping the future of both the stars and her own world.

As the chapter ends, Maya senses that the conflict is far from over, but there is a glimmer of hope. The Luminaries and the Umbra have agreed to continue the talks, and for the first time, the stars seem to shine a little brighter, as if reflecting the possibility of peace. Maya knows that the road ahead will be difficult, but she is determined to see it through, knowing that the fate of the cosmos depends on her efforts.

## Earthly Reflection

As Maya dives deeper into the role of mediator between the warring star factions, she begins to notice striking parallels between the cosmic conflict and her own life. The celestial battles, with their opposing sides, mirror tensions she's been avoiding at home—particularly a growing rift between her and her mother. The two have been drifting apart ever since Maya's father passed away, their once-close relationship strained by grief and misunderstandings.

The weight of the cosmic conflict has been overwhelming for Maya, but now, with the realization of her own personal turmoil, she feels an even greater burden. Astra, ever the guide, senses Maya's inner turmoil and advises her to address her earthly conflict with the same approach she's been using with the stars: empathy, understanding, and open communication.

Maya begins to see the cosmic conflict not just as a distant, grand battle in the skies, but as a reflection of the struggles within herself and her relationships. The Luminaries' desire for stability and the Umbra's push for change resonate with the conflict she faces at home—her mother's insistence on holding onto the past, and Maya's own need to move forward, to find a new path after the loss of her father.

At school, Maya also finds herself entangled in a conflict with her best friend, Lily. They've been growing apart, each pursuing different interests and spending less time together. The distance between them feels like a chasm, much like the divide between the Luminaries and the Umbra. The arguments and misunderstandings with Lily echo the discord in the cosmos, and Maya realizes that the cosmic lessons she's been learning can help her navigate these earthly challenges.

Determined to resolve the conflicts in her life, Maya approaches her mother first. They sit down for a heart-to-heart conversation, something they haven't done in months. Maya shares the burden she's been carrying—the pressure of mediating a cosmic war, the fear of losing her mother just as she lost her father, and the need for both of them to heal and move forward. Her mother listens, and for the first time in a long while, she opens up about her own pain and fears. They come to an understanding, agreeing to support each other in navigating their grief and finding a way forward together.

Buoyed by the success of this conversation, Maya turns to Lily. They meet at their favorite spot, a quiet park where they used to spend hours talking and dreaming about the future. Maya apologizes for the distance that has grown between them, explaining how her life has changed and how she's been struggling to find balance. Lily, in turn, admits that she's felt neglected and left out. They talk openly, just as Maya has done with the celestial beings, and realize that their friendship is worth fighting for. They make a pact to stay connected, even as their lives take them in different directions.

As Maya resolves these earthly conflicts, she notices a shift in the cosmic conflict as well. The lessons she's applied on Earth—communication, empathy, and understanding—begin to resonate with the Luminaries and the Umbra. The celestial code, once tangled and chaotic, starts to stabilize, reflecting the harmony Maya is finding in her own life.

By the end of the chapter, Maya has grown in ways she never expected. The cosmic and earthly conflicts are not just intertwined—they are reflections of each other, teaching her that the same principles of balance, empathy, and connection apply whether the struggle is in the heavens or on Earth. With these lessons in mind, Maya feels more prepared than ever to continue her role as a mediator, knowing that the battles she fights in the stars are just as much about understanding herself and the world around her.

## Deciphering the Final Code

Maya has spent weeks tirelessly working on decoding the celestial patterns. The final sections of the code have been particularly elusive, with symbols and messages that seem to shift and change, reflecting the instability of the cosmic conflict. Her nights have been filled with long hours of observation and intense concentration, and her days have been spent trying to understand the celestial messages and their implications.

One evening, after yet another frustrating session, Maya finally makes a breakthrough. The final piece of the code reveals a plan for resolving the cosmic conflict. It's a complex solution that involves both factions coming together to create a new celestial order, one where balance and mutual respect are central. The plan requires a specific celestial alignment and a ceremonial act that symbolizes the unity of opposing forces. This act will restore harmony in the universe, but it will come at a significant cost: the leaders of both factions must sacrifice their positions of power and influence, effectively giving up their roles in the celestial hierarchy.

As Maya deciphers the final code, Astra arrives to discuss the plan. Astra explains that this resolution demands not just courage but also a profound sense of selflessness. The celestial leaders have been consumed by their own desires and grievances, making the idea of relinquishing power particularly challenging. Maya realizes that convincing them to accept this compromise will be one of the most daunting tasks she has faced.

Maya's heart races as she prepares for the final confrontation. She knows that the celestial leaders, despite their flaws, have a deep connection to the stars and their roles in the universe. Convincing them to make such a profound sacrifice will be a test of her own abilities and resolve. She also understands that the success of this mission will have a direct impact on Earth. The disturbances caused by the cosmic conflict have been escalating, and resolving it is crucial to restoring balance on her own planet.

To prepare, Maya reviews all she has learned about the celestial beings, the conflict, and the final resolution. She reflects on the lessons of empathy, balance, and communication she has applied to her personal life. Armed with this understanding, she feels ready to face the celestial leaders and present the final plan.

The confrontation takes place in the heart of the cosmic arena—a majestic, otherworldly space where the factions have gathered. The celestial beings, with their luminous forms and resonant voices, are initially resistant to the idea of relinquishing their power. Maya, however, stands firm and presents the final code's resolution with clarity and conviction. She appeals to their sense of duty and their understanding of the greater good, emphasizing the necessity of their sacrifice for the restoration of universal balance.

As Maya speaks, she draws on her experiences and the empathy she has developed throughout her journey. She highlights the parallels between the celestial conflict and the earthly struggles she has faced, showing the celestial leaders that true resolution comes from understanding and selflessness. Her words resonate deeply with some of the leaders, who begin to see the wisdom in the proposed resolution.

The ceremony to enact the final plan is both beautiful and solemn. The celestial beings gather in a cosmic formation, their energies merging in a spectacular display of light and color. Maya watches as the leaders make their sacrifices, stepping down from their positions and allowing the new order to take shape. The process is emotionally charged, with the leaders expressing their final farewells and hopes for the future.

With the ceremony completed, the cosmic conflict begins to ease. The stars' alignment stabilizes, and the celestial code becomes harmonious and clear. Maya feels a profound sense of accomplishment and relief, knowing that her efforts have helped restore balance to the universe. The disturbances on Earth begin to subside, and a sense of calm returns.

As Maya reflects on the outcome, she recognizes the depth of the sacrifice involved and the courage it took to achieve this resolution. She understands that the success of the mission was not just about resolving a cosmic conflict but also about embracing the power of empathy, selflessness, and courage.

The chapter concludes with Maya returning to her own world, where she feels a renewed sense of connection to the stars and a deeper understanding of her place in the cosmos. She realizes that the final code was not just a solution to a cosmic conflict but a testament to the transformative power of sacrifice and resolution.

## Cosmic Resolution

Maya, Astra, and the celestial beings gather at the heart of the cosmic arena, where the final plan to resolve the celestial conflict is set to unfold. The once-vibrant stars now dimly flicker, reflecting the tension and uncertainty that pervades the cosmic space. Maya feels the weight of her responsibility as she prepares to guide the celestial factions through their most critical moment.

The opposing factions of stars assemble, their forms shimmering with residual discord. The celestial beings, once vibrant and commanding, now exude a more subdued light, signifying their conflicted emotions. Maya stands alongside Astra, who provides support and reassurance, reminding her of the strength and empathy she has displayed throughout her journey.

Maya takes a deep breath and steps forward, addressing the assembled factions. Her voice echoes through the cosmic expanse, resonating with a blend of authority and compassion. She recaps the resolution plan, emphasizing the necessity of compromise for the greater good of the universe. The celestial leaders listen intently, their expressions a mix of skepticism and hope.

As Maya lays out the final terms of the compromise, tensions flare between the factions. The leaders of the opposing sides voice their grievances and concerns, expressing fears about losing their influence and the potential consequences of the sacrifice. The confrontation is heated, with powerful bursts of energy and celestial phenomena reflecting the intensity of the debate.

Maya remains steadfast, using her deep understanding of the celestial code and the lessons she has learned to mediate. She addresses the concerns of each faction with empathy, acknowledging their fears while emphasizing the necessity of unity. The dialogue is emotionally charged, and Maya's resolve is tested as she navigates the complex web of cosmic politics and personal grievances.

Despite the initial resistance, Maya's guidance and persuasive arguments begin to sway the factions. The celestial leaders start to recognize the wisdom in the proposed resolution and the benefits of restoring harmony. The compromise involves a ceremonial act of unity, where both factions agree to relinquish their positions of power and work together to create a balanced cosmic order.

The ceremony is a poignant moment, with celestial beings coming together in a display of synchronized light and energy. Maya coordinates the event with Astra's assistance, ensuring that the transition is smooth and that the new order is established with grace and dignity.

As the compromise is enacted, the cosmic energy shifts from discord to harmony. The stars' alignment stabilizes, and a renewed sense of balance envelops the universe. The celestial beings radiate a harmonious glow, reflecting the restored equilibrium. Maya watches with a sense of awe and relief as the cosmic conflict comes to a peaceful resolution.

On Earth, the natural disasters and unusual celestial phenomena begin to subside. The disruptions that had plagued the planet gradually fade, and a sense of calm returns. Maya feels a deep sense of accomplishment, knowing that her efforts have helped restore balance not only to the cosmos but also to her own world.

Despite the resolution, Maya is emotionally exhausted. The journey has taken a significant toll on her, and the weight of her responsibilities lingers. She reflects on the emotional highs and lows she has experienced, from the exhilaration of discovery to the stress of mediation and the joy of resolution. Maya recognizes the profound impact the journey has had on her personal growth and understanding.

As she prepares to leave the cosmic arena, Astra offers her words of gratitude and encouragement. Astra acknowledges Maya's courage and dedication, emphasizing the importance of her role in the cosmic resolution. Maya feels a mixture of pride and weariness, knowing that her journey has come to a successful conclusion.

Maya returns to her own world, where she takes a moment to appreciate the restored balance in both the cosmos and Earth. The night sky now shines with renewed clarity, and Maya feels a deep sense of connection to the stars. She understands that her journey has not only resolved a cosmic conflict but has also transformed her own understanding of harmony and balance.

Maya's exhaustion is tempered by the knowledge that she has made a meaningful impact on the universe and her own life. As she gazes up at the night sky, she contemplates the future and the lessons she has learned, ready to embrace the next chapter of her life with a newfound sense of purpose and resilience.

## Next Chapter

Maya returns to her life on Earth, stepping back into her familiar surroundings with a sense of profound change. The once-ordinary nights spent stargazing now hold a deeper significance. The celestial code that guided her through the cosmic conflict has vanished, but its impact remains etched in her memory and heart.

Maya settles back into her daily routine, but the experiences she had in the cosmic arena have left an indelible mark on her. The ordinary world seems different, imbued with a new sense of wonder and purpose. As she resumes her studies and interactions with friends and family, Maya carries with her a quiet confidence and a renewed perspective on the universe.

The old typewriter, once a tool for deciphering the celestial code, now occupies a place of honor in Maya's room. It stands as a tangible reminder of her extraordinary journey and the stories she helped uncover. The typewriter's presence symbolizes the connection between the earthly and cosmic realms and the legacy she has inherited.

Maya occasionally sits at the typewriter, reflecting on her experiences and jotting down her thoughts. The keys that once tapped out celestial codes now serve as a medium for her reflections and personal insights. The typewriter becomes a symbol of her ongoing connection to the stars and her role in the cosmic narrative.

Maya takes time to reflect on the journey she has undergone, from the discovery of the celestial code to the resolution of the cosmic conflict. She considers the lessons learned about balance, conflict resolution, and the interconnectedness of all things. The celestial beings, Astra, and the various factions she encountered have left a lasting impression on her worldview.

During quiet nights, Maya gazes up at the stars, feeling a deep sense of gratitude and accomplishment. The stars, once distant and mysterious, now feel like old friends, their twinkling lights a reminder of the harmony she helped restore. Maya recognizes that her journey has made her more aware of the subtle influences of the cosmos on her own life.

Although the cosmic conflict is resolved, Maya understands that her journey is far from over. The stars continue to shine, each one potentially holding new stories, conflicts, and mysteries. Maya feels a sense of anticipation and readiness for whatever comes next. She knows that the universe is vast and full of unknowns, and she is eager to explore these new possibilities.

Maya's experiences have equipped her with the skills and insights to approach future challenges with wisdom and resilience. She remains open to the possibility of new celestial encounters and the continuing evolution of her role in the cosmic scheme. The knowledge that there are always more stories to uncover and conflicts to resolve motivates her to stay curious and engaged.

Maya stands on her porch, looking up at the night sky with a sense of hope and determination. The stars twinkle brightly, and she feels a profound connection to the cosmos. The journey she has undertaken has changed her forever, but it has also opened doors to new adventures and possibilities.

Maya understands that her role in the universe is part of a larger, ongoing narrative. The celestial code may have disappeared, but its essence remains within her. She is ready to embrace the next chapter of her life, knowing that the stories of the stars are far from over and that her journey as a cosmic storyteller is just beginning.

* * * * *

# MEMORY ARCHITECTS

## The Perfect Memory

The late afternoon sun filtered through the sleek glass walls of MemoraTech's headquarters, casting an ethereal glow over the cutting-edge technology and polished surfaces. Sixteen-year-old Zoe Bennett stood at the entrance of the company's high-tech lobby, her heart racing with a mix of excitement and nerves. Today was her first day as a junior memory architect, a job she had dreamed about ever since she learned about the futuristic possibilities of memory manipulation.

Zoe's introduction to the world of MemoraTech began with a grand tour of the facility, guided by Ethan, the charismatic project manager. Ethan, with his impeccably styled hair and confident stride, led her through corridors lined with holographic displays showcasing the company's latest projects.

"Here at MemoraTech, we don't just create memories; we craft experiences," Ethan explained, his tone as smooth as the sleek floors beneath them. "From reliving your happiest moments to experiencing dreams you've never had, we make the impossible possible."

Zoe followed him into the training room, where she met her new team: Lucas and Mia. Lucas, the tech-savvy programmer, was hunched over a workstation, his eyes fixed on a flurry of code scrolling across multiple screens. He barely looked up as Zoe entered, offering a distracted wave.

Mia, on the other hand, greeted Zoe with a warm smile. "I'm Mia," she said, her voice soft and welcoming. "I handle the artistic side of things—making sure the memories are as vivid and emotionally resonant as possible."

The room was filled with the hum of machinery and the occasional beep of notifications. Zoe's training began with a deep dive into the technology behind memory creation. She learned about the sophisticated neural interfaces that allowed for the encoding and implantation of memories, and how the company's advanced algorithms ensured that every memory felt authentic and tailored to the client's desires.

Her first assignment seemed straightforward—a routine task involving the creation of a nostalgic memory for a high-profile client. Zoe was excited to put her training into practice. She was assigned to review and finalize the memory before it was implanted into the client's neural interface.

The memory was designed to allow the client, a wealthy entrepreneur named Mr. Reynolds, to relive a cherished childhood summer at his family's beach house. Zoe loaded the memory file into her workstation and began her review.

At first glance, everything seemed in order. The sun-drenched beach, the laughter of children, and the gentle crash of waves all appeared flawlessly recreated.

But as Zoe delved deeper, she noticed something strange. There were discrepancies in the memory—details that didn't match the client's request. An old-fashioned radio on the beach, for instance, was playing music that wasn't popular during the time Mr. Reynolds was supposed to be reliving. The shadows in the memory seemed to flicker unnaturally, and the emotional intensity was slightly off from what Zoe had been taught to expect.

When Zoe brought these anomalies to Ethan's attention, he brushed them off. "It's probably just a minor glitch," he said with a dismissive wave. "We have bigger issues to deal with. Don't worry about it."

But Zoe's curiosity was piqued. The discrepancies seemed too deliberate to be mere glitches. As she continued to investigate, she discovered hidden layers within the memory file—encrypted data that suggested unauthorized alterations. The implications were troubling. What if someone was manipulating memories for purposes beyond what was intended?

Late into the evening, Zoe found herself alone in the training room, her gaze fixed on the glowing screen. The anomalies in the memory file were starting to form a pattern—one that hinted at something larger and more sinister than she had initially imagined. The office was quiet, the only sounds were the soft hum of machinery and her own steady breathing.

As the shadows lengthened outside and the city lights began to twinkle, Zoe felt a growing sense of unease. The memory she had been assigned to finalize was more than just a simple task—it was a piece of a puzzle that, when put together, might reveal a hidden truth about MemoraTech and the world of memory manipulation.

Zoe staring at the screen, a mix of excitement and apprehension in her eyes. She knew that uncovering the truth behind the anomalies would not be easy, and that it might challenge everything she thought she knew about her job and the world around her. But one thing was certain: her journey had only just begun.

## Hidden Code

The sterile lights of the MemoraTech office cast long shadows across the rows of workstations as Zoe returned late that evening. Her mind was abuzz with the anomalies she had uncovered in Mr. Reynolds' memory file. The discrepancies were nagging at her, and she couldn't shake the feeling that there was something more sinister beneath the surface.

Sitting alone at her workstation, Zoe scrutinized the memory file once more. The encrypted data she had found wasn't just random errors—it seemed like a deliberate insertion. Her fingers danced over the keyboard as she tried to decode the hidden layers of the file, using the knowledge she had gathered during her training.

After hours of painstaking work, Zoe managed to extract a series of alphanumeric sequences from the encrypted data. They resembled a code, but its meaning was still unclear. Exhausted but determined, Zoe decided to seek help. She turned to Lucas, the tech-savvy programmer, who was known for his knack for solving complex problems.

"Lucas, I need your help with something," Zoe said, approaching him the next morning. "I've found something unusual in one of the memory files. It looks like there's a hidden code embedded in it."

Lucas raised an eyebrow, his interest piqued. "Hidden code? That sounds interesting. Let's take a look."

They worked together in Lucas's dimly lit corner of the office, surrounded by a maze of cables and screens. Zoe explained the anomalies she had noticed, and Lucas began analyzing the extracted code. His eyes widened as he deciphered the sequences, realizing that the code wasn't a glitch but a carefully crafted insertion.

"This is definitely not an error," Lucas said, his voice low and serious. "The code is sophisticated—someone has gone to great lengths to hide it. And if it's embedded in memory files, it could mean that we're dealing with something far more dangerous than a simple malfunction."

Zoe nodded, her heart pounding. "What do you think it's for?"

Lucas shook his head. "I don't know yet. But if there are other files with similar irregularities, it might be part of a larger scheme. We need to investigate further."

As the team began to notice more irregularities in various memory files, the sense of unease grew. Mia, who had been working on creating emotional content for a series of memory experiences, reported inconsistencies in the emotional responses of the memories she was crafting. Ethan, the project manager, was increasingly irritable and evasive whenever the team raised concerns.

"We've got a pattern here," Lucas said one evening, showing Zoe and Mia a compilation of anomalies across different memory files. "These inconsistencies aren't random. They suggest that someone is manipulating the data deliberately."

The team's investigation led them to uncover evidence of manipulated memories involving high-ranking officials and powerful corporations. The memories had been altered to cover up scandals, influence public perception, and even blackmail individuals into compliance. The realization was chilling—MemoraTech was not just a company creating memories but a key player in a web of deceit and corruption.

"We're in the middle of something big," Zoe said, her voice trembling. "If this goes public, it could ruin lives and shake the foundations of powerful institutions. But if we don't act, it could mean the end of our own safety."

Lucas agreed. "We need to be careful. The people behind this are powerful and ruthless. If they find out we're onto them, there could be serious consequences."

Zoe, Lucas, and Mia knew they had to uncover the full extent of the conspiracy and expose the truth. But they also understood the risks involved, as their actions could have far-reaching consequences both for themselves and for the world at large. The discovery of the hidden code had opened a Pandora's box, and the path ahead was fraught with danger and uncertainty.

## Shattered Illusions

The once-familiar hum of the MemoraTech office now seemed oppressive as Zoe, Lucas, Mia, and Ethan huddled around their workstations, the weight of their findings pressing heavily upon them. The more they uncovered about the memory manipulation conspiracy, the more it seeped into their personal lives, shaking the very foundations of their identities.

Mia, the talented memory artist known for her meticulous attention to detail, was the first to crack under the strain. She had always prided herself on crafting perfect memories, blending emotions and experiences into seamless narratives. Yet, as she delved deeper into the conspiracy, she stumbled upon discrepancies in her own past memories.

"Something's not right," Mia murmured, her hands trembling as she stared at her monitor. "I've been cross-referencing some of my old work, and there are inconsistencies. Memories I thought were real—were they altered? Did I even experience them the way I remember?"

Zoe, who had been working closely with Mia, glanced up from her own screen. "Mia, are you saying you think your own memories have been tampered with?"

Mia's eyes were wide with fear. "I don't know. But if this is happening to us, how do we know what's real anymore? What if our entire understanding of our lives is based on manipulated memories?"

Lucas, who had been poring over the technical data, looked up with concern. "If our memories can be altered, then we can't trust our own perceptions. It's not just about the memories we're creating for clients—it's about our own sense of self."

Ethan, usually the calm and collected project manager, was increasingly showing signs of paranoia. He paced the room, his face flushed, and his eyes darted nervously. "This is getting out of hand. We're uncovering things that could make us targets. What if they've already messed with our memories to make us forget something crucial?"

The emotional strain began to take its toll on the team's relationships. Disagreements erupted over the smallest issues, and trust, once a strong bond between them, now felt fragile and uncertain. The team's unity was crumbling under the pressure of their investigation.

Zoe found herself torn between her growing doubts about the authenticity of her own memories and her desire to help her friends through their crises. She tried to offer reassurance, but her own fears about her reality were too overwhelming.

One evening, as the team gathered in the break room for a rare moment of respite, Mia broke down. "I don't know what's real anymore," she sobbed. "How do we fight a conspiracy when we don't even know who we are?"

Ethan's anxiety reached its peak as he struggled to maintain control. "We have to stay focused. If we start doubting everything, we'll never uncover the truth."

Lucas, despite his own reservations, tried to ground the team. "We need to keep our wits about us. The more we question our own memories, the less effective we'll be in our investigation. Let's focus on the facts we've gathered and use them to piece together the conspiracy."

As they continued their work, the team realized that their investigation was not just about exposing the conspiracy—it was also about confronting their own fears and uncertainties. The realization that their memories and identities could be at risk made the stakes even higher. They were no longer just uncovering hidden truths; they were grappling with their own shattered illusions.

In their quest for answers, they discovered that the conspiracy ran deeper than they had imagined. The more they uncovered, the more they understood that their own realities were intertwined with the very conspiracy they sought to expose. The chapter closed with the team feeling disoriented and fragmented, their sense of self shaken as they faced the daunting challenge of separating truth from manipulation.

## Conspiracy Revealed

The muted glow of the office lights seemed to cast a shadow over Zoe, Lucas, Mia, and Ethan as they gathered around their workstation, the gravity of their findings weighing heavily on them. The initial fragments of the conspiracy had evolved into a horrifying revelation: MemoraTech, their employer and supposed leader in ethical memory manipulation, was at the epicenter of a dark scheme to control influential figures through memory alteration.

Lucas, his face a mixture of disbelief and determination, adjusted his glasses as he reviewed the latest data. "We've traced the anomalies back to several high-profile clients and discovered a disturbing pattern. It's not just random alterations—these are deliberate modifications aimed at manipulating decisions and actions."

Zoe leaned in, her heart pounding. "Are you saying that someone within MemoraTech is orchestrating this?"

Mia, her eyes scanning the documents with growing concern, nodded. "Yes. The patterns point to directives coming from the top. Mr. Carter, our boss, is implicated in this. He's been using our technology to influence key individuals and shape outcomes in favor of the corporation's interests."

Ethan, his anxiety giving way to a steely resolve, slammed his fist on the table. "If Carter's behind this, it's not just a corporate scandal—it's a threat to every person who's been manipulated. We have to expose him, but how?"

Lucas continued, "We need concrete evidence to bring this to light. But we're under constant surveillance, and any wrong move could tip them off."

The team exchanged glances, the enormity of their task settling in. They were not only up against a powerful entity but also facing the danger of being discovered and discredited.

As they began formulating a plan, Zoe took the lead in devising a strategy. "We need to gather evidence discreetly. I suggest we access secure files that have the most direct links to the alterations. We'll have to be careful—anyone watching will be looking for us to slip up."

Mia, who had always been the most meticulous, volunteered to create a diversion. "I can handle the office systems. I'll create a plausible reason for us to access restricted areas and gather the necessary files."

Lucas offered to handle the technical side, setting up encrypted communications to ensure their discussions remained private. "I'll monitor their surveillance systems and try to find blind spots we can exploit."

Ethan, despite his earlier paranoia, took on the role of coordinating their efforts and ensuring they stayed on track. "We need to stay united. This is bigger than any of us individually. If we're going to pull this off, we have to trust each other completely."

The team worked with renewed purpose, each member playing a critical role in the operation. As they delved deeper into the conspiracy, they faced numerous obstacles. Their every move seemed to be monitored, with their activities coming under scrutiny from Mr. Carter's network of spies.

One evening, as Mia prepared to access a secure database, alarms went off. The team scrambled to cover their tracks and avoid detection. Lucas's skills were put to the test as he deflected intrusions into their encrypted communications.

Despite the constant danger, the team managed to gather crucial evidence linking Mr. Carter and MemoraTech to the manipulation scheme. They compiled records, communications, and data that clearly illustrated the extent of the conspiracy.

The team preparing to unveil their findings. They knew that exposing the conspiracy would put them in direct conflict with powerful forces, but their commitment to justice and the truth fueled their resolve. As they faced the looming confrontation, they understood that their actions could either dismantle the corrupt system or lead to their downfall. The stakes were higher than ever, and the path to uncovering the truth was fraught with peril.

## Memory Vault

The hum of the server room was eerily silent as Zoe, Lucas, Mia, and Ethan stood before a hidden access panel in a secluded corner of MemoraTech's underground facility. The walls were lined with advanced security systems, and the air was thick with tension. They had just discovered the location of the secret memory vault, a repository rumored to contain the most damning evidence of the conspiracy they were trying to expose.

Zoe's hands trembled slightly as she worked on bypassing the high-security lock. "This is it," she whispered, glancing nervously at her team. "If we get through this, we'll have everything we need to expose the truth."

Lucas, eyes glued to his laptop, monitored the vault's security feed. "I'm seeing multiple layers of encryption and biometric locks. This is going to be tricky. We need to be quick and precise."

Mia took a deep breath, her face illuminated by the glow of her tablet. "I've prepared a diversion in the system to create a temporary security lapse. It won't last long, but it should give us a small window of opportunity."

Ethan paced back and forth, his earlier anxiety replaced by a focused determination. "Once we're in, we need to grab as much evidence as we can. No matter what happens, we can't leave empty-handed."

With a final, decisive keystroke, Zoe disabled the security lock. The panel slid open with a faint hiss, revealing a narrow corridor leading to the memory vault. They moved cautiously, their footsteps echoing in the dimly lit corridor.

The vault door loomed before them, a massive steel barrier adorned with a complex array of security features. Zoe, Lucas, and Mia worked in tandem to override the final security measures. Lucas tapped away at his laptop, decoding the biometric locks while Mia interfaced with the vault's internal systems.

"Almost there," Lucas muttered, sweat forming on his brow. "Just a few more seconds."

The vault door creaked open, revealing a vast room filled with rows of memory storage units, each one humming with life. The walls were lined with sleek, high-tech devices, and the air was filled with a faint, electronic buzz. Zoe's heart raced as she took in the sight.

The team moved quickly, accessing the memory units and downloading data onto portable drives. Each file they uncovered contained manipulated memories—images, experiences, and emotions that had been altered to serve the corporation's agenda. The depth of the conspiracy was even greater than they had imagined.

"Look at this," Mia said, her voice tinged with shock. "These memories—this isn't just about controlling individuals. They're altering key events, shaping public perception, and manipulating entire narratives."

Ethan scrolled through the files, his face growing grim. "These memories show everything from political manipulations to personal vendettas. This isn't just corporate greed; it's a deliberate attempt to control and deceive on a massive scale."

As the team continued their search, alarms suddenly blared. The security system had detected their intrusion, and the vault's automatic lockdown had been triggered. Panic set in as red lights flashed and a deep, mechanical voice announced that security personnel were en route.

"Time's up," Zoe said urgently. "We need to get out of here, now!"

The team scrambled to gather the last of the evidence and fled the vault. They navigated the maze-like corridors of MemoraTech, avoiding security patrols and surveillance cameras. Their hearts pounded as they made their way back to their makeshift hideout, the weight of their discovery pressing heavily upon them.

Back in the safety of their hideout, the team reviewed the files they had managed to retrieve. The evidence was overwhelming and damning, but they knew that exposing it would put them in grave danger.

"We have what we need," Zoe said, her voice filled with determination. "Now we just have to figure out how to get this information to the public without getting caught."

Lucas, though exhausted, nodded. "It's going to be risky, but we can't let this go on any longer. The truth needs to come out."

Mia, her earlier confidence shaken but not broken, added, "We've come this far. We can't stop now."

The chapter ended with the team preparing for the final stages of their mission, knowing that the path ahead would be fraught with danger and uncertainty. They were on the brink of exposing a conspiracy that could change everything, but they also understood the risks they faced. The battle for truth and justice was far from over, and their resolve would be tested in ways they had never imagined.

## Betrayal

The dimly lit room of the hideout was filled with tension as the team gathered around a table cluttered with documents, portable drives, and laptops. The atmosphere was electric with anticipation. Zoe, Mia, and Ethan were finalizing their plans to leak the incriminating evidence they had uncovered. The weight of their discovery had set them on a path to expose the corruption within MemoraTech and the broader conspiracy.

Lucas was at the corner of the room, ostensibly working on the final preparations. His demeanor seemed oddly distant, but the team attributed it to the stress of their situation. They had no reason to suspect anything amiss—until it was too late.

"Are we ready?" Ethan asked, glancing at Lucas. "This is our last chance to get everything right."

Lucas, his face expressionless, replied, "We're ready. Just give me a moment to finalize the upload."

As the team busied themselves with the last-minute checks, Lucas's phone buzzed on the table. Zoe noticed that he had been receiving a series of encrypted messages.

Her curiosity was piqued, but before she could ask, Lucas's demeanor abruptly changed. He stood up, his face pale and strained.

"There's been a change of plans," Lucas said, his voice tight. "We need to hold off on the leak."

The team looked at him in confusion. "What are you talking about?" Mia demanded. "We don't have time to waste."

Without warning, Lucas's phone rang. He answered it quickly, his eyes darting around nervously. "Yes, Mr. Carter. Everything is in place," he said, his voice betraying a note of fear.

The realization hit Zoe and the others simultaneously. Lucas's betrayal was not just a personal fail; it was a critical blow to their mission. Zoe's heart sank as she watched Lucas's face contort with guilt and resolve.

"Lucas, what's going on?" Zoe demanded, her voice shaking with anger.

Lucas's shoulders slumped, and he finally met their eyes. "I'm sorry. I've been working for Mr. Carter all along. I was ordered to sabotage your plans. I didn't have a choice."

Mia's face reddened with fury. "You've been feeding information to the enemy? You betrayed us!"

"I didn't want to," Lucas pleaded. "But they've threatened my family. I didn't know how to—"

Before Lucas could finish, the door to their hideout burst open, and a group of security personnel stormed in. Lucas's betrayal had led to their location being compromised. Panic erupted as the team scrambled to gather their things and escape.

"Get the evidence!" Zoe shouted, grabbing the portable drives and shoving them into a bag. Ethan and Mia covered their retreat, fending off the security personnel with makeshift weapons.

Lucas, torn between guilt and fear, tried to help, but his actions were clumsy and ineffective. The team managed to slip out through a side exit, their hearts pounding as they fled through the darkened streets.

Once they were safely hidden in an abandoned building, the team collapsed in exhaustion. The weight of Lucas's betrayal hung heavily in the air, and the once-unbreakable bond between them felt shattered.

"How could you do this to us?" Ethan asked, his voice strained with emotion. "We trusted you."

Lucas, sitting apart from the group, looked devastated. "I'm sorry. I thought I could find a way out without hurting anyone. I was wrong."

Mia, tears streaming down her face, shook her head. "You've put us all at risk. We could have been caught."

Zoe, feeling a mix of anger and sorrow, spoke up. "We need to decide what to do next. We've lost a lot, and we need to figure out how to proceed without Lucas's help."

Lucas, his face pale and resigned, nodded. "I understand. I'll do whatever I can to make it right. Just—please be careful. They're coming after you now."

The team was left to grapple with the fallout of Lucas's betrayal. The trust they had once had was severely damaged, and the path forward was uncertain. They had escaped with the evidence, but the cost of their mission had grown exponentially.

As they prepared for their next steps, the team realized that their fight for truth had become even more dangerous. They would need to rely on their remaining strength and resolve to see their mission through, knowing that every move they made would be fraught with peril.

## Public Exposure

The team, now more resolute than ever, gathered in the dimly lit conference room of their temporary hideout. The evidence they had risked so much to obtain was secure, and their next move was crucial: they needed to ensure the truth about MemoraTech's conspiracy reached the public.

Maya sat at the center of the room, surrounded by Ethan, Mia, and an independent journalist named Ava Reynolds. Ava was known for her investigative work and had the connections and resources needed to expose the conspiracy to the masses.

"Alright, we're ready to move forward," Ava said, spreading out a series of documents and data files on the table. "The first step is to get this information into the hands of the public before they can suppress it."

Mia, still shaken by the recent betrayal, looked up. "We've seen what they're capable of. How do we make sure this gets out?"

Ava's eyes were steely with determination. "I've set up a press conference for tomorrow. We'll leak the evidence to major news outlets and provide them with the documentation needed to substantiate the claims. But we need to be prepared for pushback."

Zoe, clutching a folder of the most sensitive information, nodded. "What's our plan if they try to stop us? We've already seen what they're willing to do."

Ethan, ever the strategist, added, "We should anticipate legal threats and attempts to discredit us. We need to be ready to defend our position and stay one step ahead."

The team spent the rest of the evening preparing for the press conference, ensuring that every piece of evidence was correctly compiled and that their statements were clear and compelling. As dawn broke, they made their way to the venue, a large auditorium that had been booked for the public revelation.

Inside, the atmosphere was electric with tension. Reporters, photographers, and curious onlookers filled the seats, buzzing with anticipation. Ava took the stage, flanked by Zoe, Mia, and Ethan. The crowd hushed as Ava began her opening statement.

"Ladies and gentlemen, today we have a story that reveals a disturbing truth about the manipulation of memories and the misuse of technology," Ava announced. "We are here to expose the extent of a conspiracy involving MemoraTech, a corporation that has been altering and controlling memories for its own gain."

Zoe, feeling the weight of the moment, stepped forward to present the evidence. As she displayed documents and screenshots, the audience began to react with a mix of shock and disbelief. The data was irrefutable, and the gravity of the conspiracy became apparent.

However, just as the presentation was gaining momentum, a commotion erupted at the back of the room. Security personnel, hired by Mr. Carter and MemoraTech, began to disrupt the press conference. They attempted to seize the evidence and intimidate the reporters.

"Stop them!" one of the security guards shouted, pushing through the crowd.

Panic ensued as chaos erupted in the auditorium. Ethan and Mia sprang into action, working to protect Ava and the evidence. Zoe, determined not to let the truth be silenced, grabbed a live microphone and addressed the crowd.

"This is the truth!" Zoe shouted. "They're trying to stop us because they don't want you to know what's really happening!"

The media, sensing a major story in the making, began to record the confrontation. Despite the attempts to shut them down, the footage of the chaotic scene and the evidence presented became a sensation.

Outside the auditorium, the team regrouped, their hearts pounding from the adrenaline and fear. Ava, now surrounded by journalists, was answering questions and clarifying the details of the conspiracy.

"We've done it," Ethan said, his voice filled with both relief and exhaustion. "The evidence is out there, and people are starting to take notice."

Mia, still processing the ordeal, nodded. "But we need to stay vigilant. They won't give up easily."

As they left the venue, the team could see the impact of their efforts. News outlets were broadcasting the story, and social media was ablaze with discussions about the revelations. The public was demanding answers, and pressure was mounting on MemoraTech and its affiliates.

Despite the victory, the team knew that their fight was far from over. The powerful forces they had exposed would not take kindly to being challenged. As they faced an uncertain future, they remained determined to see their mission through, knowing that the struggle for justice was just beginning.

## Aftermath

The aftermath of the press conference was a whirlwind of activity and change. News outlets continued to cover the scandal surrounding MemoraTech, and the public outcry against the corporation was unprecedented. The company faced severe backlash, with government investigations launching into their practices and top executives, including Mr. Carter, being called to account for their actions.

Zoe, Ethan, Mia, and Ava found themselves at the center of this storm, their lives altered forever by their brave decision to expose the truth. The team was celebrated by some as heroes but faced legal challenges and personal threats from those who sought to discredit or intimidate them.

Zoe sat in her small apartment, now filled with piles of legal documents and media clippings. The stress of ongoing legal battles and the constant media scrutiny had taken its toll. She glanced at the framed photo of her and her team from their earlier days at MemoraTech, a bittersweet reminder of how far they had come.

Mia, though relieved that the truth had been revealed, struggled with the personal impact of their actions. The public revelation had triggered an introspective journey for her, as she grappled with the betrayal of her own work and the ethical implications of memory manipulation. She spent her evenings at a local café, writing reflections and journal entries about her experiences and the personal growth she had undergone.

Ethan had become the face of the campaign for accountability. His charismatic nature and eloquence in interviews had made him a prominent figure in the media. Despite the recognition, he found himself dealing with the stress of constant public scrutiny and the burden of leading the charge for reform. He continued to work closely with Ava, helping to organize support for new legislation aimed at regulating memory manipulation.

Ava, whose investigative prowess had been crucial in exposing the conspiracy, faced her own set of challenges. She became a respected figure in journalism but also faced threats from those who wanted to silence her. Her role as a mediator between the team and the public became increasingly demanding as she navigated the complexities of the media landscape.

One evening, the team gathered at a small park near their old office building. The place was now a symbol of both their triumph and the trials they had endured. The sky was clear, and the stars shone brightly, a comforting reminder of their journey.

Zoe addressed the group, her voice filled with a mix of relief and contemplation. "We've been through so much, and our lives have changed in ways we couldn't have imagined. But we did what we set out to do. We uncovered the truth and fought for what's right."

Mia nodded, her eyes reflecting the starry night. "It's been a tough road, but I feel like we've grown stronger through this. We've learned a lot about ourselves and each other."

Ethan, looking at the horizon, added, "We've faced incredible challenges, but knowing that we've made a difference makes it all worth it. We've restored some integrity to personal memories and exposed the dangers of unchecked power."

Ava, always the realist, said, "There's still a lot of work to be done. The battle against corruption and misuse of technology continues, but we've set a precedent. Our actions have started a conversation about the ethics of memory manipulation and the importance of transparency."

As they shared their thoughts, the team reflected on the impact of their actions and the changes they had brought about. The revelations had led to significant reforms in the industry and had inspired others to question the ethical boundaries of technology.

Despite the personal and legal repercussions they faced, Zoe and her friends found solace in their shared experiences. They had fought against a powerful corporation and had emerged with their integrity intact. The journey had tested their resolve and their relationships, but it had also forged a bond that would remain strong as they continued to navigate their futures.

The team knew that their fight for justice was far from over, but they took comfort in the knowledge that they had made a meaningful difference. Their efforts had preserved the integrity of personal memories and had set a new standard for accountability in a world where memories could be bought, sold, and altered. As they looked to the future, they remained committed to their cause and to each other, ready to face whatever challenges lay ahead.

## New Reality

As the dust settled from the exposure of MemoraTech's conspiracy, society began to shift towards a new era of awareness and regulation. Stricter regulations on memory manipulation were enacted, and new ethical guidelines were put in place to ensure that such technology would be used responsibly. The once-shadowy world of memory manipulation was now under scrutiny, and efforts to restore public trust in the industry were underway.

Zoe found herself at the forefront of this movement. Her role in the conspiracy's exposure had earned her a position with an ethics board dedicated to overseeing memory technology. She used her firsthand experience to help shape the new regulations, working tirelessly to ensure that the technology would serve society in a way that honored individual autonomy and integrity.

Her office, decorated with both personal mementos and symbols of her fight for memory rights, was a hub of activity. She conducted workshops and wrote articles advocating for ethical practices, striving to create a world where memories were treated with the respect they deserved.

Mia, having come to terms with the complexities of her role in memory creation, shifted her focus to counseling and support for those affected by memory manipulation. She worked with individuals who had undergone memory alterations, helping them to piece together their experiences and find closure. Her deep empathy and understanding made her a valued asset in this new role, and she found fulfillment in helping others navigate their personal journeys.

Ethan, with his media background, continued to champion transparency and accountability. He became a prominent voice in public discussions about the ethical use of technology, using his platform to highlight the importance of oversight and integrity. His involvement in various advocacy groups allowed him to influence policy changes and foster a culture of responsibility within the tech industry.

Ava, now a renowned investigative journalist, used her skills to explore new stories and expose ongoing issues related to technology and ethics. Her work continued to challenge powerful entities and hold them accountable. Despite the risks, she remained committed to uncovering the truth and ensuring that technology served the public good.

The team remained closely connected, often meeting to discuss their progress and support each other in their respective roles. Their shared experience had forged a bond that went beyond mere friendship. They understood each other's struggles and triumphs in ways that only those who had fought the same battles could.

One evening, they gathered at a park overlooking the city, the skyline a testament to the changes they had helped bring about. The night was clear, and the stars—once a symbol of their struggle—now seemed to shine with renewed hope.

Zoe looked around at her friends, her heart full of gratitude. "We've come a long way from those days at MemoraTech. I never imagined we'd be here, but we've made a difference."

Mia nodded, her gaze fixed on the city lights. "We've learned so much about ourselves and each other. It's been a journey of growth and discovery."

Ethan, always the optimist, added, "The work isn't over, but we've set a new standard. We've shown that it's possible to use technology responsibly and ethically."

Ava, reflecting on their journey, said, "Our fight has led to real change. We've faced incredible challenges, but we've made sure that the future of memory technology is brighter and more transparent."

As they talked, Zoe realized that their journey had not only changed their lives but had also laid the groundwork for a more ethical approach to technology. Their fight against manipulation had sparked a movement towards greater accountability and respect for personal memories.

The road ahead was filled with both challenges and opportunities. The team knew that the battle for ethical technology would continue, but they were prepared to face it with the same determination and unity that had brought them this far.

Zoe continued to advocate for memory ethics, Mia supported those affected by memory manipulation, Ethan promoted transparency, and Ava pursued investigative journalism. Together, they faced the future with hope, knowing that their efforts had made a meaningful impact.

As they looked up at the stars, Zoe felt a profound sense of purpose. The memory of their journey—both the trials and the triumphs—would guide them as they moved forward. They understood that while their fight against manipulation was far from over, they had set the stage for a more transparent and ethical future.

The new reality they faced was one of rebuilding and recovery, but it was also a testament to their resilience and commitment. Their shared experiences had not only changed their own lives but had also contributed to a world where memories were valued and protected. And with that, they embraced the future, ready to continue their journey towards a better tomorrow.

* * * * *

www.ingramcontent.com/pod-product-compliance
Lightning Source LLC
Chambersburg PA
CBHW032012150726
47990CB00005B/1934